E.J. RUSSELL

THE
HOUND
OF THE
BURGERVILLES

QUEST INVESTIGATIONS
BOOK TWO

The Hound of the Burgervilles
Copyright © 2021 by E.J. Russell

Cover art: L.C. Chase, http://lcchase.com
Edited by Meg DesCamp

ISBN: 978-1-947033-35-1

First edition
November 2021

Contact information:
ejr@ejrussell.com

E.J. RUSSELL

THE
HOUND
OF THE
BURGERVILLES

QUEST INVESTIGATIONS
BOOK TWO

Dedicated to my readers who wanted more from Matt (and Jordan),
and to Sir Arthur Conan Doyle, despite my disappointment that he never really believed in giant spectral hounds.

CHAPTER ONE

"Are you sure about this?"

I glanced sidelong at Eleri, my new Quest Investigations co-worker and self-described BFF, as we inched closer to the counter in Wonderful Mug Coffee Shop. If I looked straight at her, she'd know I was about to lie, big time. Apparently I have a tell: My lips are moving.

"One hundred percent," I said. Yup. Total lie. Ninety percent, maybe. Okay, seventy-five. *Fine.* Fifteen at the most.

Or ten.

To be honest, guilt niggled at my insides over asking Eleri to accompany me. Since she's fae, she has free access to Faerie through any available gateway. My Quest credentials entitle me to use the FTA—Fae Transportation Association—to travel between any relatively secluded spots via shortcuts through Faerie, but there were a couple of reasons why I couldn't justify calling up Frang, my usual driver, and toddling off through the portal.

First, I didn't feel right using a Quest FTA voucher for this trip, since it was personal, not professional.

Second, FTA drivers follow carefully regulated paths through Faerie so the traffic won't disturb the residents, and none of them would ever take me where I needed to go. Because everyone—even a duergar like Frang, who's as big as your average commercial refrigerator and regularly knocks back shots of dragon piss and crushed holly berries—steers clear of bean-nighe.

I expect you would too, because you know, Washerwoman of Death and all.

I know what you're thinking: Don't do it, Hugh! Or, if you're *really* trying to get my attention: Don't do it, Matt! Because when you use my actual name instead of my Quest Investigations moniker, I know you mean business. But come on, cut me a break, okay?

After three weeks of nothing but texts with Lachlan Brodie, the selkie who was actually interested in dating me, I was running seriously short on patience. We'd agreed not to go any further until he wasn't married anymore, but—

Oh. Right. Did I mention that my prospective boyfriend is still married? Well, he is. Technically. And since I'm not a home-wrecker and Lachlan isn't a cheater, both of us refused to so much as kiss until he severs the handfasting knot with his fae husband.

And I really, *really* wanted to kiss Lachlan Brodie.

"When we get there," I said as we crept toward the cashier, "let me do the talking." Grizel, the bean-nighe I was seeking, would answer three questions for us if we went about it properly, but she was *extremely* literal about what constituted a question.

If Eleri were a wolf or bear shifter rather than a dryad, I'd have described the noise she made as a growl. "I don't know why we have to go to a stupid coffee shop, anyway. Zeke always has a fresh pot of the best coffee in the known universe back at the office"—she lowered her voice—"with druid-blessed beans."

"We're at the coffee shop because I know better than to try to get any sense out of you before you've had your first cup. And this morning's trip—"

She smirked. "You don't want anyone at work to know about it, do you?"

I shot her a glare. "*You* know."

"Yes, but I'm your BFF. You tell me everything."

"Not *everything*," I grumbled. Some things were too embarrassing to admit. Like how following years of pining after one unattainable man, I'd shifted my affection to another man who was just as unattainable. At least at the moment. "And when did you become my BFF?"

"Are you saying I'm not?"

I frowned, thinking over the very short time since I'd met Eleri on my first solo case for Quest. She'd been working as a maid then and wearing a severe black and white uniform, with an attitude to match. After our somewhat rocky start, we'd become close in a remarkably short time. Now she was comfortable flying her true self around me: a style favoring clunky boots, patterned leggings, denim skirts, and a rainbow's worth of sweaters and jackets—"In *natural* fibers," she'd informed me with a sniff—as well as more snark than any other ten people. "I...guess not."

"There you go. So what's the deal?"

We shuffled forward again. "It's been three weeks," I murmured.

She fluttered her eyelashes at me. "Since we declared our undying friendship for each other?"

"Since Lachlan said he wanted to date me."

"Oh, brother." She rolled her eyes. "Are you telling me we're running a stealth mission in Faerie today because you want to get laid?"

"Shhhh!" I glanced around wildly. Wonderful Mug was located a stone's throw away from United Memorial Hospital, which had a wing devoted to treatment for the supernatural races—supes, they called themselves—not that any humans other than me would ever know about it, since it sort of existed in an alternate dimension.

Consequently, any one of the bleary-eyed people currently queued up for their morning caffeine fix could be a supe. But the Mug was popular with humans too, and the supe community had strict rules about exposing their existence to *my kind* in a way that would draw unwanted attention and interference. Aside from the dire punishments on deck for violation of the Secrecy Pact, I had no desire for anybody—supe or human—to know about today's little jaunt.

In case you hadn't caught on already, it wasn't exactly legit.

"We're going," I said, "because Lachlan—and okay, me too—shouldn't have to wait forever for Wyn to surface." Considering Lachlan's soon-to-be-ex was a Corlun Dwr, a Welsh water sprite, *surface* might be a literal description. For all anyone knew, he could be lounging around at the bottom of a lake somewhere. "And Wyn should know that it's safe for him to come out of hiding."

She tilted her head, her eyes going unfocused for a moment. "That's fair. But I still don't know why we have to keep it so quiet we couldn't even use the translocation gate at the office. We'd get to Faerie much quicker and have druid-blessed coffee and scones to boot. If Lachlan hired us to find Wyn..." She studied my face and trailed off. "He didn't hire us, did he?"

I winced. "Not *technically*. But he hinted that he would if Wyn didn't come back soon."

"So what's the rush?"

"The rush?" I narrowed my eyes at her. "How old are you?"

She stuck her nose in the air and sniffed. "It's impolite to ask that."

"Why? Because I should never ask a *lady* her age? That's a little sexist, isn't it?"

"It's got nothing to do with *gender*. The only real way you can determine a dryad's age is by counting our rings." She bared her teeth. "After we're dead."

I gulped. "Oh. Well. Never mind. But I'm guessing you're older than you look."

"How old do I look?"

"Maybe late twenties?"

"Damn," she muttered. "I was hoping for twenty-one, max."

"Don't be vain. You know you look good." She did. Eleri was lithe and petite, her golden-brown hair in a pixie cut, her skin smooth and light brown—except when she was manifesting a tree, when it turned distinctly bark-like. "Not a day over sapling."

"Shut up," she said, but her smile glimmered.

"My point is that all of you..." I made a rolling gesture with my hand to indicate I was referring to supes in general. "You're all *extremely* long-lived. Lachlan and Wyn have centuries to work out their issues. I'll be lucky if I have another good decade or so—and trust me, as a human, I won't carry my age nearly as well as you do."

"Ah," Eleri said. "Also fair. Okay, I'm on board."

"Thank you," I replied as we finally made it to the counter.

"Good morning, Hugh." Sierra, the cashier, winked at me. Since she ran my credit card for my orders, she knew my name was really Matt Steinitz. But I used Hugh—what everybody at Quest called me—as my Mug name, since nobody ever gave their real name to the baristas. "The usual?"

"Yes, please. And a hazelnut latte, extra whip, for my friend."

Sierra grinned at Eleri, who blinked in a rather dazed way. "What name should I use for you?"

"Uh..."

What the heck? I peered down at Eleri. She was *never* at a loss for words. I glanced between her and Sierra. Oh. *Oh*. "Flora," I said. "You can call her Flora."

Eleri shot me a wild-eyed glance and swallowed. "Flora. Flora works."

We moved aside to wait for the new barista to fix our drinks. Until last summer, the regular morning barista had been a supe —an *achubydd*, a magical healer—although he was so deep in hiding that nobody knew. Heck, he didn't even know he was working next to a hospital that was practically Supe Central. Jordan, Quest's werewolf "intern," had once wreaked his particular brand of chaos at the shop too, but now, as far as I knew, Wonderful Mug was staffed by humans only.

Which would be as much a problem for Eleri if she was, er, *interested* in Sierra as it was for me with Lachlan.

"You realize she's human, right?"

Eleri shot me a fulminating glare. "I'm aware, thank you. But since we're about to embark on a very sketchy secret mission so you can get busy, I'd suggest you keep your comments to yourself."

"Right." I saluted. "Sorry. Carry on with the ogling."

"Shut *up*."

We collected our coffees and left the Mug, Eleri casting only a few longing glances over her shoulder at Sierra. Sierra returned longing for longing and glance for glance. *Very interesting.* We'd *definitely* be returning to the Mug, and I doubted Eleri would complain about it next time. In fact, she'd probably suggest it.

She led me to a pocket park a few blocks from the hospital. I glanced around curiously. The place had a footprint hardly bigger than the Quest offices, but the mature trees—both evergreen and deciduous sporting brilliant autumn color— along with ranks of rhododendrons cut off the view of the street. "Is this a regular FTA stop?"

"Nope. But I'm a citizen of Faerie, and since the King and Queen loosened the barriers, I've got pretty much global access as long as I enter near a tree. Hell, I could *be* an FTA driver if I wanted to pick up extra gold. In fact—" She took the last swig of her coffee and pitched the empty purple cup into the park's lone trash bin. "—I almost decided to go that route after I ended the gig at the Martinsons. If Quest hadn't offered me a job, I wouldn't have had many other options." She wrinkled her nose. "I'm not big on the whole gardening scene. That's one of the reasons my clan chief disapproves of me."

"That guy," I said with disgust. "Mr. Stick-Up-His-Ass. How is he still in charge?"

She shrugged. "He's OG."

"Old guard?"

"Old growth. It's impossible to uproot him." She grinned, her incisors more pointed than most humans. "Although that doesn't mean we don't try." She plucked my cup out of my hand and sent it after her own.

"Hey! I wasn't finished with that!"

"You want to get laid or not?"

"Eleri," I said, my tone laced with warning. "That's not what this is about." Mostly. Okay, mostly, but not *entirely*. Lachlan didn't deserve to have his life put on hold, either.

"Whatever. Let's go."

She grasped my wrist and hauled me after her between the trunks of two maple trees and then...

My breath caught, just as it did every time I made that transition between my world—the human world—and Faerie. Everything was different here. It *smelled* different. Newer and older at the same time, which sounds weird, I know, but it's the only way I can describe it. The only fuel burned in Faerie was wood, and not even much of that, since the trees are practically sentient. Magic is the real power source. So there's always a hint of ozone, like after a thunderstorm, but otherwise everything just smells so fresh and, I don't know, *green*.

And the sky. Well, it's not blue. Or not only blue. It's the color spectrum: Red in the morning and violet at night, moving through all the other colors as the Faerie day—which may or may not be the same as an Outer World day, since time moves differently there—progresses. Niall, one of my bosses, and the brother of the Faerie King, once explained that it was because Faerie was an artificial construct, created by the elder gods in the Days Before (don't ask "before what?" or you'll get *that look* and the very unhelpful response of "before Faerie"). He suggested I think of the whole thing as being enclosed in a soap bubble or a glass ball, its surface acting like a prism.

I suspected there was more to it than that, but it was still so freaking *cool*. I was literally in another dimension, one where magic was ordinary and gender was optional and anything could happen.

Since I'd wanted to get this little task taken care of as soon as possible—and before Niall and Mal, our other boss, noticed Eleri and I weren't in the office—the sky was still red, maybe tinging toward orange. We were at the foot of the tor. The ceilidh glade where most of the big gatherings happened was inside the grove of trees at the top. The Keep—the big stone monstrosity that used to be the seat of the Unseelie King before the consolidation of the Seelie and Unseelie courts and the marriage of the Seelie Queen and Niall's brother—was off somewhere on the other side of the tor. Although given that Faerie geography wasn't exactly static, who knew where it was today.

"Which way?" Eleri asked.

"Uh..." Good question. I'd only encountered this particular informant once before, and I'd been in company with Mal at the time. I pointed up the side of the tor, a little to the left of center. "That way. I think."

Eleri shot me an exasperated glare. "You *do* know where we're going, right?"

"Cut me a break. Do *you* know where everything is in here?"

"Well. Yes." She pressed a hand below her heart, over her *calon*, the extra organ that every supe possessed—except vampires, apparently. "I can call on the One Tree and it will show me where anything is. It's how the FTA drivers can navigate the regular paths."

"Oh. Right. Um... I'm looking for a stream."

She upped her exasperation by a factor of ten. "Well, *that's* specific. This place is lousy with streams."

"With a tree above it."

"Dude," she said. "Seriously?" And she gestured to the vista that was literally nothing *but* trees.

"Where someone hangs washing."

She stilled. "Are you *kidding* me? You're looking for *Grizel*?"

I lifted my chin in an attempt to look confident. "She'll be able to tell us where Wyn is."

"If you're lucky," she retorted, "and can translate whatever cryptic crap she hands you. You'd be better off consulting a freaking crystal ball."

I blinked. "You've got those?"

She screwed up her face. "Well. No. But playing pin the tail on the centaur would be more dependable than Grizel."

"I don't care," I said. "She helped us find another missing person once, so I'm willing to try again."

She folded her arms. "But not to tell Mal or Niall about it, or ask for their help."

"It's not their problem. It wouldn't be fair."

She sighed. "Fine. It's your funeral pyre." She squinted at the tor, scanning for something that I couldn't detect. "There."

She took off up the hill with me slogging along behind her. The tor was one of those changeable Faerie geography things— sometimes it could feel like you were scaling Mount Everest and other times it wasn't any more strenuous than hiking over the Nike campus berm. Today it was somewhere in the middle, so by the time we got to the top and stopped inside a dense grove of alder and birch, I was breathing heavily, but not about to pass out. Eleri, of course, looked as fresh as she had in the line at Wonderful Mug, although considerably more awake.

"Grizel's stream is through there." She pointed at what appeared to be a solid wall of tree trunks.

"How the heck are we supposed to get the lay of the land? I may be a surveillance specialist, but I can't see through that."

She shrugged. "So move the trees."

It was my turn to give her the *Seriously?* glare. "Now is not the time for dryad humor, Eleri."

"For a change, I'm not joking."

"Fine. I'll bite. How the heck do I get trees to move?"

"Ask them nicely." For an instant, she maintained her poker face, but then she relented and grinned at me. "Chill, BFF. I've got you." She strode forward and placed one palm on a birch, the other on a neighboring alder, murmuring something I couldn't hear clearly but which sounded like Welsh.

And the trees moved aside.

"Damn. You're good," I said.

Eleri just winked at me and gestured for me to follow her. We crept through the magically less dense copse until we could peer out through the underbrush to the hillside beyond.

Grizel was there, all right, in all her blue-skinned glory. And when I say blue, we're not talking about faint bluish undertones. Nope, we're talking full on Smurf. She wasn't tall—probably a hand-span shorter than Eleri who barely topped five feet—although her knot of iron gray hair, held in place by some kind of bone, added another inch or three. She was wearing the same ankle-length green skirt and faded, loose-knit shawl that she'd been wearing the first time I'd seen her, so either she only had one set of clothes or she had a really consistent fashion sense.

On the other hand, if you were called the Washerwoman of Death, who knew how you handled your own laundry?

Several garments already hung from low-hanging branches of the gnarled oak tree about halfway down the slope. She had a couple of clothespins gripped between her teeth as she lifted a limp shirt out of the wicker basket at her feet.

"Uh oh," Eleri murmured. "Somebody's number is up."

"Let me do the talking, okay? She can be really literal about what constitutes a question, and we can only ask three." I'd been formulating them for the last week, turning them over in my mind to make sure they couldn't be interpreted more than one way, and I was convinced I had them nailed. Wyn was as good as found already, and then Lachlan and I could get on with, well, getting it on. "Just block her access to the stream as fast as you can because if she makes it into the water, she doesn't have to answer." And once we tipped our hand, our chances of successfully ambushing her again would be precisely zero.

"I'm not an idiot," Eleri hissed. "I know how this works."

"Okay. You head for the stream and I'll herd her toward you. But she's quicker than she looks, so don't dawdle."

"Don't worry," she said, lowering into a sprinter's crouch. "If I can outrun a forest fire, I can outrun her."

"Ready. Set. Go!"

We launched ourselves out of the trees, Eleri speeding toward the stream bank while I angled toward Grizel. She saw me—I know she saw me, because she stared right at me—but she didn't do anything other than spit out the clothespins and bare an alarming array of pointed yellow teeth.

Uh oh. I remembered something from our first encounter— she'd believed I'd been some kind of tribute, a gift to her from Mal, in exchange for information.

Maybe tackling her without his backup wasn't my most brilliant notion.

I started to slow my pace, but before I could veer off to the side, something streaked past me, clipping my hip and sending me staggering into the laundry.

While I was wrestling with a face full of wet suede—*ewww*— Grizel shouted a curse in Gaelic. When I finally pulled the clinging fabric off my head, she was charging down the hillside, a lean wolf with a telltale white blaze on his flank nipping at her heels.

"Jordan," I groaned. "Of course it had to be Jordan."

The young werewolf had started interning at Quest at the same time Eleri hired on, and he was nothing if not enthusiastic. Unfortunately, he didn't possess a lot of common sense and if he'd ever considered the consequences of his actions before he plowed full steam ahead, I'd never heard about it.

Eleri was crouching at the stream's edge, her arms spread, her fingers sprouting leaves and her signature thorn accessories, a resolute expression on her face. While Grizel hadn't run from me, Jordan, as reckless as he was, was getting the job done of driving her toward Eleri. Okay, this might work out after all.

But then Grizel reached into the pocket of her apron, and her arm flew in a windup any major league pitcher would envy.

"Fetch!" she called.

Jordan's gaze immediately snapped to follow the trajectory of whatever she'd sent sailing through the air and he took off after it, crashing through the underbrush in his eagerness.

Grizel cackled, then calmly strolled the last few yards toward the stream, neatly bypassing Eleri who, for some reason, didn't try to stop her. Grizel stepped into the water on extremely large bare blue feet, then turned to smirk at us.

"Safe," she said. "Tha great ninnies."

CHAPTER TWO

I peeled the wet suede off my chest and glared at Eleri. "Why didn't you stop her?"

Eleri glared back. "Because she *rooted* me!"

I glanced down at Eleri's feet—or where her feet should have been, except she was up to her ankles in the sod. I blinked. "She can do that?"

"Apparently," Eleri muttered, flexing her knees and obviously trying to free herself from the ground.

Grizel folded her arms under her shelf-like bosom. "I can protect mysen." She snorted and squinted up at me as I stumbled down the bank. "Did tha learn nowt when tha was here last, tha great gowk?"

"We just wanted to ask some questions," I said.

"Then happen tha should *ask*. Nicely. And don't return unless tha art prepared to bide. Forever." She turned and sloshed away down the stream, leaving her laundry basket behind.

Well, *that* wasn't ominous. I heaved a sigh. "I don't suppose your tree whispering would work with a bean-nighe?"

Eleri pointed to her buried feet. "What do you think?"

"A point. How long do you suppose—"

"Hey, um, guys?"

We both turned at Jordan's tentative call from the bushes. Well, I turned, but Eleri couldn't do more than twist partway around.

"Jordan," I said, "what are you doing here?"

He poked his head between the glossy leaves—which I really hoped weren't the Faerie equivalent of poison oak or ivy, because it was clear from the glimpses of white skin amid the foliage that he was naked. "Helping?" he said, a hopeful note in his voice.

"Where are your clothes?" I asked resignedly.

"Oh. Next to the snack vending machine back at the office." He smiled sunnily. "I figured out how to use that translocation gate on the fourth floor."

I sighed. "Then you should probably shift again so you're not mooning Faerie on the way back to the office."

"I *can't!*" he wailed. "As soon as I picked up that stick, I morphed, like, *instantly,* and I can't call my wolf up anymore." He blinked, in full-on puppy-dog-eyes mode. "You don't think it's *permanent,* do you? It's like I'm *human.*"

"Oh, the horror," I said dryly.

"Sorry, Hugh," he muttered.

"It's fine." Well, not fine, not by a long shot. Not only hadn't I gotten the answers I needed from Grizel, but now I had a rooted dryad BFF and a naked werewolf sidecar. Clearly getting to work on time was off the table: I could hardly leave Eleri here alone, and escorting Jordan through Faerie in his birthday suit would be decidedly awkward, especially if we exited in the same park where we entered.

I glanced at the damp jerkin in my hand. Wearing a dead—or soon-to-be dead—man's clothes wouldn't be *my* favored fashion statement, but what choice did we have?

Grizel had hung several garments on the tree before we arrived, so I stalked back up the hill and unpinned the sole pair of trousers...leggings...whatever. "Soggy leather," I grumbled, "wonderful." I took them over to Jordan and handed them to him along with the jerkin. "Put these on."

He wrinkled his nose. "*Ewww.* They're *wet.*"

Jordan had a canine love-hate—mostly hate—relationship with water, but once again, he didn't have many options unless he opted for a leaf loincloth. "And you're naked. Unless you want to parade out of Faerie and through Portland with your bare bits flapping in the chilly breeze, you'd best get over yourself."

He bit his lip, pink staining his cheeks, and I felt a little bad about my harsh tone. "Sorry, Hugh." He plucked the clothes out of my hand.

I sighed again. "It's okay. But why are you here, anyway? Aren't you supposed to be helping Zeke at the office?"

Jordan had begun "interning" with us after the owner of Wonderful Mug had strongly suggested the coffee shop wasn't the best place for him to work after way too many accidents with and to the milk steamer. He was enthusiastic and eager, but not exactly skillful. Mal and Niall, our bosses, had assigned him to work with our demon office manager, figuring that after navigating the hellish landscape and complicated politics of Sheol for centuries, one junior werewolf wouldn't be a stretch for Zeke to handle.

And maybe an ordinary junior werewolf wouldn't have strained Zeke's patience or abilities. But we're talking about Jordan. I was surprised poor Zeke hadn't pulled out every one of his curls by now.

"Zeke's been training me on the phone system, but I'd much rather be out in the field with you." Jordan pulled the jerkin over his head. It was so big on him that it nearly reached his knees, although it clung clammily to his body. Jordan wasn't exactly small—he was a coltish, lanky guy, and just in the time I'd known him, he'd inched taller than me—but whoever the clothes belonged to must be built along mythic proportions, close to Frang's size.

Frang. Could these be *his* clothes?

My fingers went numb. *No. Please, no.* I really hoped Grizel wasn't hanging Frang, er, out to dry as it were. He was gruff and rough-hewn, but I liked to think he was a friend. I peered at the jerkin and breathed a little easier. I didn't remember ever seeing Frang wear suede with that complicated embroidered pattern on the breast. Not exactly a fan of decoration, Frang. He even gave me the side eye when I wore a striped button-down instead of one of my usual black T-shirts.

"So." I had to clear my throat to get the words out. "You followed us because you were bored? How did you even know where we were going?"

Behind me, I heard a squelchy *sluuuurp* and a muffled "Thank the Goddess," from Eleri, who must have finally uprooted herself. Good. Because as cool as Faerie was, I was more than ready to get the hell out of it at the moment.

"I heard you talking about it," Jordan said, his voice muffled because he had his head down, trying to find a way to keep the trousers from sliding down his lean hips. Resignedly, I unbuckled my own belt and handed it to him. I had enough padding around the middle that I didn't have to worry about my jeans heading south.

Eleri joined me next to the bush. "But we never discussed it at the office."

He peeked at us from under his lashes. "But you did at the falafel restaurant the other day. And at the Mug this morning."

Eleri and I gazed at one another, wide-eyed. "Did you know he was there?" I asked.

"Not a clue," she answered.

"Score!" Jordan beamed at us. "I was *shadowing* you. So I could learn how to do the job. And since neither of you saw me, I'm good at it, right?" He emerged from the bushes, looking like a toddler dressed in his father's clothes. "So can you tell Mal and Niall that I'm ready to be an investigator instead of an office go-fer?"

The idea of Jordan on his own on a case made my blood run cold. "Jordan, tailing somebody when they don't know about it isn't shadowing. It's stalking."

His face fell. "It is?"

"Yep."

"But isn't that what you do when you're on a surveillance job?"

"Uh..." I glanced at Eleri for support.

She shrugged. "I got nothin'."

"Come on," I said tiredly. "Let's get back to the office." I gestured to Eleri to precede us. "After you, Ms. All Access Faerie Pass."

As we followed her back down the tor, Jordan picked irritably at the jerkin. "This is really nasty. It wouldn't be so bad if it was dry, but—"

"Maybe remember this the next time you're tempted to shift and leave your clothes behind," I said as I dodged around a scatter of rocks the size of soccer balls.

He blinked at me. "But I always leave my clothes behind."

"This far behind? As in another freaking dimension?"

"Oh. Well. No. I guess that was a mistake, huh?" He beamed at me, apparently having no trouble navigating the rough terrain despite being barefoot. "I'll do better next time."

Eleri tapped her forest green Doc Martens against a boulder next to an enormous oak tree, dirt clods pattering onto the ground. "Next time? Goddess give me strength." She marched past the tree and disappeared.

"Guess that's our exit cue," I said to Jordan. "Come on."

I'd expected her to lead us back to the little pocket park near Wonderful Mug, but instead we stepped out into the fourth floor corridor of the Quest offices.

"Hey!" Jordan said. "There's my clothes." He trotted over to a tumbled pile of fabric in front of the soda machine as I grabbed Eleri's elbow and towed her in the other direction.

"What the hell, Eleri?" I whispered. "I wanted to keep this whole fiasco on the down-low. Kind of hard to do if we—"

"If we what?" She cocked a slanted eyebrow at me. "Arrived the way we usually do?"

It was my turn to blink. "Oh. Good point."

She patted my arm. "Don't worry, Hugh. Your secret is safe with me." She jerked her chin at Jordan, who was attempting to pick up his clothes without letting them touch his damp borrowed finery. "I doubt Jordan will mention it either."

"Are you kidding?" I muttered as we headed for the stairs. "When have you ever known Jordan to be discreet about anything? He'll probably confess the minute he spots Mal." I glanced back at Jordan, who was trying to juggle cell phone and clothing as he shuffled after us. I leaned closer to Eleri. "I think he still has that crush."

"Nah," she replied. "He's shifted his affections to Rusty Johnson, remember?" She grinned. "Apparently Rusty wielding a sledgehammer feeds all of Jordan's Thor fantasies."

I chuckled a little tightly, since I couldn't exactly throw stones —Lachlan's Jason Momoa-as-Aquaman vibe had hooked me the first time I'd seen him. But then I frowned. "Do you hear that?"

She glanced around. "Hear what?"

Before you ask why I didn't snark at Eleri about *listening* instead of *looking* for the sound, let me remind you: I was human. She wasn't. For all I knew, some supes *could* see sound waves. I mean, Eleri could talk to trees, for Pete's sake, so it wasn't outside the realm of possibility. "The phones," I said. "They haven't stopped ringing since we got here."

"I haven't worked here that long," she said, low-voiced. "Is that unusual?"

I nodded. Since Quest didn't get that many phone calls—our prospective clients tended to prefer to show up in person or contact Mal or Niall directly—the sound was peculiar enough. But Zeke was super efficient and operated with demon super speed, so this many unanswered calls raised more than a few red flags.

I took a couple of steps down, my treads in counterpoint to the persistent ringing. "Jordan, what did you do to the phones before you left to stalk us?"

He looked up from his cell phone. "I was *shadowing* you," he said indignantly. "And I didn't do anything!"

"No?" I jerked my thumb downward toward the second floor lobby. "So suddenly we're busier than an OPB pledge break?"

He screwed up his face. "Well... I did try this call forwarding thing so the answering service would pick up while I was in the field."

I took a deep, calming breath. It didn't work. "We don't have an answering service."

He blinked again. "We don't?"

"No. Quest is the equivalent of supe security, investigative, and emergency services. We answer every call." That is, Zeke answered every call. And what he didn't catch, Mal or Niall did. I wasn't sure whether to be relieved or insulted that I wasn't part of the phone tree.

"Well, something's wrong with the phone system then, because half the calls I've answered in the last three days have been nothing but dead air, and the other half were looking for animal control." He frowned. "I figured somebody from my home pack was pranking me." He rolled his eyes. "Animal control. Very funny. Very *mature*."

"Come on." I hitched my camera bag strap onto my shoulder more securely. "Whatever you did is obviously making Zeke's life miserable and possibly losing Quest business, so let's figure it out."

"Oh. Right." He plucked at his wet tunic again. "Could I change first? This is really uncomfortable. And the pants keep riding up my...um..." His gaze slid to Eleri and he flushed.

"Fine." I shooed him toward the fourth floor restroom. "Go ahead."

"I'll return your belt as soon as I change, Hugh, promise." He bolted down the hallway.

Eleri shook her head. "It's hard to remember he's actually twenty-one. He seems so much younger."

"You can't wonder why werewolf packs ship their juniors off to Howling Residences until their prefrontal cortex develops a little more and they learn how to navigate the human world. Imagine a whole litter of Jordans."

She shuddered. "Don't. I'll have nightmares of being bombarded by hundreds of Frisbees while trying not to trip in a field full of holes."

We hurried downstairs and into the lobby to find Zeke poking button after button on the multi-line phone, his headset askew.

"Hello, Quest— Damn it. Quest Investi— Hello? Hello?" He slumped in his chair. "I don't understand it. I can't connect any of these calls."

I watched the lights chase from one line to the next like the countdown to a stock car race. "I think Jordan may have created an endless forwarding loop."

"What?" Zeke frowned down at the console. "I didn't know that was possible." He tore off his headset and disappeared under his desk. A moment later, all the lights on the console went dark. They stayed out for a count of three, then all lit up at once before going back to normal.

Zeke crawled out from under his desk and plopped back in his chair. "Thank goodness."

I grinned at him. "When in doubt, reboot, eh?"

He smiled back. "You've taught me well, Hugh." The phone rang again and all of us froze. Zeke gingerly donned his headset and pressed the blinking button, his shoulders almost level with his ears. "Good morning. Quest Investigations. How may I help you?" He relaxed a bit, although a frown puckered his forehead. "I'm sorry, but I'm afraid you have the wrong number." He hung up.

"Let me guess. Animal control?"

Zeke nodded. "Yes. How did you know?"

"Jordan said he's been getting those calls for the last three days, interspersed with dead air calls. He thought it might be someone from his home pack pranking him."

Zeke shook his head. "I don't think so. I've been getting similar calls—well, not the animal control, but the hang-ups—for a couple of weeks. I..." He bit his lip and flinched, glancing over his shoulder as if he was afraid somebody was behind him. He had reason. When he first left Sheol as part of the demon work-release program, he'd been monitored 24/7 by an AI—an angel interface—and the angel in question was a total douchecanoe who never missed a chance to abuse poor Zeke. "I thought it might be my old Sheol supervisor. He lost a lot of status after the Realm Accords passed, not to mention the drop in his income since he didn't..."

"Didn't have you to shake down for money anymore?" I said softly. The AI hadn't been the only one who'd abused Zeke. I still couldn't understand how anybody could treat anyone as sweet as Zeke so poorly. Luckily, he had his boyfriend, Hamish, as well as all of us at Quest at his back now.

"Exactly." The phone rang again. He smiled ruefully as he answered.

"Matthew."

Even if I didn't recognize that deep voice with its delicious Scots accent, only one person called me *Matthew*, pronouncing it *MattHugh*, a combination of my actual human name—Matt—and the name I went by at Quest—Hugh.

I turned, and there, silhouetted by the window, was Lachlan Brodie, uncrowned king of the selkies, and my (unfortunately) still-married not-quite-boyfriend.

CHAPTER
THREE

"Lachlan," I croaked. "I didn't know you were coming into town." Lachlan lived on his boat out at the coast. If I'd known he was planning to stop by today, I wouldn't have staged my stealth mission to Faerie. I, uh, kind of hadn't told him that I was trying to locate Wyn.

His smile glinted in his tanned face, framed by his gold-highlighted brown hair. "Thought we'd surprise you. Invite you to join us on a wee cruise."

"We? Us?" I glanced around wildly. Had *he* located Wyn? But then I noticed the kid in the rainbow beanie peeking out from behind Lachlan's broad-shouldered form. "Blair. Hi."

I was a little confused. The Quest security spells were configured to keep humans out, so how had Blair slipped in? Maybe they slid through in Lachlan's wake, considering the wide swath he cut through virtually everything—land, sea, and my consciousness. Or maybe if a human was accompanied by a supe, there were exceptions? I made a mental note to ask Zeke about it later.

Blair waggled their fingers at me, smiling shyly, although their gaze never reached my face. I noticed that even though they were still wearing their oversized army surplus jacket, the sweater underneath was a brilliant scarlet rather than the nondescript gray from our last meeting, and it fit a heck of a lot better, as did their obviously new jeans. They were also sporting a pair of bright yellow wellies.

I was still wearing my usual North Face fleece jacket, which was probably why Blair could recognize me (other than Lachlan's greeting, of course).

Blair had prosopagnosia. Facial blindness. So they couldn't recognize people's faces unless they had really, really prominent features. I...didn't. Ordinary old Matt Steinitz—aka Hugh Mann—that was me. Medium height, medium brown hair, medium brown beard scruff, nothing remarkable in my build. But for some reason, big, beautiful Lachlan Brodie was interested in me.

I'd heard it from Mal, from Zeke, from Eleri, that I ought to be careful: Male selkies were like catnip to humans, so my reaction to Lachlan might be nothing more than a response to his innate species charm. But that didn't explain Lachlan's fascination with *me*. And after wasting years yearning for a man I couldn't have, who didn't want me as anything other than a friend, I wanted to see where this went.

Behind me, Zeke said, "I'm sorry, but you have the wrong number. No, this isn't animal control." Clearly Jordan needed to have a chat with his pack mates. And if that didn't work, I'd ask Mal to have a chat with them. That'd be enough to scare them out of a couple years' growth.

"Going to introduce me?" Eleri said brightly.

I squinted at her, suspicious. "I believe you know Lachlan. You once went tree of heaven with bonus thorn accessories on his ass."

She rolled her eyes. "I don't care about *him*. But he's not alone, is he?"

What was she...oh. She must recognize Blair as human—she and her fellow rebellious dryads had certainly pegged me as one the first time they saw me—and realized that we needed to shield any supernatural shenanigans from sight or risk violating the Secrecy Pact.

I think I've mentioned the Secrecy Pact to you before. No supe can reveal the existence of the community to a human under pain of death and untold destruction. Literally.

I'm not talking about accidental random sightings that could be chalked up to imagination or variations in human sensitivity. Those can be excused. But intentional, extensive exposure? Nope. No way. Absolutely zero tolerance.

Except for me. I was a special case—the only human allowed full *participative* access to supe society. But I didn't want the kind of fallout that I'd suffered before I'd been vetted to fall on Blair. Poor kid had enough to deal with.

"Eleri, this is Blair. Blair, this is Eleri."

She held out her hand. "Hugh's best friend. Pleased to meet you. I love your boots."

Blair glanced up at Lachlan, who nodded encouragingly. Then they reached out and shook with Eleri quickly before snatching their hand behind their back. "They're new." As usual, Blair didn't look at Eleri's face, but they did study her Doc Martens. "You've got dirt on yours."

"Yeah." Eleri's smile didn't even waver. "I've been gardening." Not a flinch, not a side-eye, not a single tell. Eleri was a much better liar than I was. It's why she was able to work undercover as a maid for a homicidal fire mage for months with no one the wiser.

Lachlan cleared his throat. "Blair and I have been shopping. The new boots, the sweater. Raincoat, too, but that's in the truck." Lachlan rested a huge hand on Blair's shoulder and the kid gazed up at him worshipfully. I could definitely relate. "Blair's signed on to crew for me now and again this winter on some of my fishing charters, but they couldn't do that without proper kit."

Clever Lachlan. He'd found a way to upgrade Blair's wardrobe without alerting their father or bruising their pride. If I knew Lachlan—and despite our brief acquaintance, I had a better bead on his character than on my own sometimes—he'd probably store all the new clothes on his boat so Blair would have them when needed.

"That's great," I enthused.

Eleri nudged me with an elbow. "Why don't you and Lachlan have a chat while I take Blair up to check out the vending machines?"

I blinked at her stupidly. "What?"

"Have a *chat*," she said through a tooth-gritted smile. "With *Lachlan*. In your *office* so you don't bother Zeke."

I glanced at Zeke, who'd just answered another call. "Hello? Hello? Is anybody there?"

"Oh. *Oh!*" I laughed weakly. "Right."

She gestured to Blair. "Which do you like best—potato chips, raisins, or Snickers?"

Lachlan patted Blair's shoulder. "Nothing too salty, jo."

"I know," they said, with a typical preteen eye-roll. "Are there any M&Ms?" They sighed. "Plain, not peanut."

"Absolutely," Eleri said brightly. If there weren't now, there would be by the time the two of them got up to the fourth floor. The Quest spells didn't only handle security. They also covered the care and feeding of the staff. Magic was so freaking cool. "Any food concerns other than salt?" Eleri asked Blair, but flicked a glance at Lachlan.

Blair shook their head, but Lachlan said, "Stay away from the Mountain Dew, Blair."

The kid rolled their eyes again. "I *know*."

Eleri didn't offer to take Blair's hand as she gestured for them to come upstairs—she was pretty perceptive for somebody who was occasionally a tree.

"So," I said, rubbing suddenly damp palms against my jeans. "Want to check out my office?"

"I do," Lachlan purred suggestively.

"It's up one flight. This way."

He placed one hand on the small of my back as we headed out of the lobby toward the stairs, sending a *zing* from my heels to the top of my head. *Dammit.* Behind us, I heard Zeke say almost testily, "No, I'm sorry, but I've told you before. This is *not* animal control."

My office wasn't particularly fancy, and it sure as heck wasn't large. With a man the size of Lachlan crowding in with me, it felt no bigger than a shoebox. If I were smart, I'd retreat behind my desk so there'd be something more than a few inches of charged airspace between me and his really broad chest, narrow hips, long legs, and...and...

And ring finger that didn't sport a wedding band but might as well.

I'd be the first to admit that I wasn't the brightest bulb in the chandelier, but I was starting to get the hang of emotional self-preservation, thank you very much. I ducked behind the desk.

Lachlan lifted one eyebrow—the one with the thin white scar bisecting it. "Running from me, are you, Matthew?"

I could lie, but what was the point? "Yes."

Now, Lachlan Brodie could be the grumpiest cuss on the planet—I believe I'd mentioned that?—but when he smiled like that, I was surprised the office wasn't further crowded with fluffy woodland creatures, unicorns, and songbirds. "I won't do anything either of us would regret. You know that. As long as I'm still married to Wyn, we'll have to keep things..." He glanced around my office, from the desk with its oversized monitor to the orderly shelves with research materials and camera equipment to the Aeron chair that Zeke had ordered for me practically the minute Quest had taken over the offices. "Safe for work."

"I know." Lachlan had told me up front that he wouldn't cheat, that he never broke a promise, and I believed him. I also hadn't been completely honest with him about my own personal, er, entanglements. "There's something I need to tell you."

There went that eyebrow again, and I had to brace myself against my desk because my knees went weak. I'd never pegged myself as someone with an eyebrow kink, but that was before I met Lachlan. "Is it that you and your dryad best mate took a little jaunt into Faerie to pose a question or two to a certain bean-nighe?"

I blinked at him, my jaw sagging. "What? How—"

"How did I find out?" He chuckled and edged toward the corner of the desk as if he couldn't help himself. "Time runs at a different pace in Faerie, so word's got around. I may only be fae by marriage and admitted to Faerie because of the fae/selkie reciprocity agreement, but I still hear the gossip, and Grizel's a Scot." His gaze was intense, but I couldn't tell whether he was angry or...something else. "I don't attend to it often, but when it involves someone I...care about? Then I listen."

My shoulders slumped and I swallowed thickly. "You know I was there to ask her about Wyn, then?"

"Wyn?" His eyes widened. "Is that why you trespassed on her hillside, disrupted her business, and sent her into a right strop? To ask about Wyn?"

"Of course." I frowned at him. "Isn't that what you meant about gossip involving someone you care about?"

He chuckled, a warm, rolling sound that resonated in my chest. "I meant *you*, lad. Tongues are wagging about *you*."

I didn't want to think about tongues in connection with Lachlan, because that would only remind me that we hadn't kissed yet—and apparently wouldn't for the foreseeable future. "Oh."

His expression sobered. "But Matthew, you mustn't put yourself at risk like that. Not for me. Grizel has a fancy for humans that she's not been allowed to indulge since their majesties outlawed, shall we say, *involuntary* Faerie residency? But if a handsome bloke presents himself to her of his own free will? She's not the sort to resist temptation."

I probably had hearts floating in my eyes. "You think I'm handsome?" I croaked.

"If that's the only thing you culled from that warning—"

"No. It's not. I realized it was probably a stupid plan when I came face to face with her, but I didn't make the trip only for me. It was for you, too. Until you and Wyn sever the knot—"

"The two of *us* can't move forward." He reached out but dropped his hand before he touched my face. "I'm impatient too. But Wyn's not a cruel man. He won't leave me hanging forever."

I moved behind my chair, needing the extra barrier between us. "But that's the thing. Your forever and mine are very different. You said time runs differently in Faerie. I've heard that before too—faster out here than in there. What if Wyn just thinks he's taking a long weekend or a little vacay before surfacing from whatever river or lake he's chilling in, but when he emerges from Faerie, it's been fifty years?" I gripped the chair back. "I'm human, Lachlan. I don't have the luxury of time that you supes do."

He rubbed one big hand across his face. "Ah, lad. You don't —"

"But that's not what I wanted to tell you."

He stilled, eyes narrowing. "It's not?"

"No." I swallowed. "The thing is... Um..."

"Out with it," he growled. "You've got me primed for the worst. Don't leave me hanging."

"The thing is, I'm not entirely footloose myself."

His brows drew together in a scowl. "You're not?" His gaze flicked to my bare left hand. "You're not married too?"

"No! God, no. But see, the thing is..." I swallowed, my mouth dry. "I've been in love with someone for a couple of years now."

He crossed his arms, his sea-green anorak doing nothing to mask the bulge of his biceps. "Years, is it?"

I nodded. "At least."

Then he seemed to deflate. "Ah. I'll not stand in your way, lad."

"No!" I barked again. Jeez, I sounded like a two-year-old. "That's not it. He doesn't want me. He never did. He only saw me as a friend, and he's married now, anyway."

He looked a little more hopeful. "Is it your job? You can't make it work with another human when you have to hide so much from him?"

"He's, uh, not human." I smiled weakly. "Grizzly shifter. His husband is an incubus."

"Incu—" Both Lachlan's eyebrows shot up this time. "Goddess bless, you're in love with Ted Farnsworth? The bloke who runs the Wildwood resort?"

I nodded miserably. "*Was* in love. Might still be. I don't know." I met his gaze squarely. "I want to give the two of us— you and me—a chance. But what if I can't get over Ted? What if the pull I feel toward you is just…selkie charm? I want to *know*. I want to *try*. But we can't. Not until you're free. And even when you are…"

He smiled gently. "Your heart might not be ready."

"Yeah. That."

He beckoned to me with both hands. "Come here, lad." When I hesitated, he chuckled. "Don't worry. Even friends can indulge in a hug now and again, and you look as though you could use one."

I shouldn't. Should I? Oh hell. Sue me. I'm weak. But I hadn't been touched like that for longer than I could remember, so I edged out from behind the desk and into his arms.

It felt…incredible. Like being enfolded in the biggest, warmest, softest blanket in the world—although there was nothing about Lachlan that was remotely soft. He was all hard muscle, and I carefully ignored something else that was hard, as difficult as it was to miss.

"Nobody can ever say for sure how two people—or more, if that's their joy—will fit together," Lachlan murmured. "If we find we don't suit? It won't be the first time for me, and it sounds like it won't be the first time for you either." He dropped a soft kiss on the top of my head. "All we can do is try. Learn about each other. Spend time with each other. Let events play out as they will." He lowered his head to whisper in my ear. "I promise by the heart of the sea that I won't let our time run out."

I shivered. Lachlan never broke his promises, and when any selkie invoked the heart of the sea, it was doubly binding. "Okay," I said, my voice muffled against his chest. "I can live with that."

Lachlan pulled back—*dammit!*—and gazed down at me, his eyes hot. "Shite, Matthew. I want to—"

A knock sounded at the door and we leaped apart like we were both on fire—which, come to think of it, wasn't too far off the mark.

"Hugh?" Zeke called. "Niall's in his office. He'd like to speak with you and Eleri."

My belly dropped. This couldn't be good. "I'll be there in a minute."

"Make it a short one," Zeke said, his tone apologetic even through the heavy oak door. "He said immediately and I don't think he's inclined to wait. If you—" Somebody else called, too faint for me to make out. "What?" Zeke's voice was muffled, so he was probably facing the other speaker. "Jordan, that can't be — Wait, all right? Don't do anything." His sigh was clearly audible. "Hurry, Hugh." There were no footsteps, but then, Zeke might not have touched the ground when he sped away. Demon anti-grav was another of his abilities—he could literally float through the air, and after Lachlan's promise, I wasn't sure I wasn't a foot or so above the ground myself.

As much as I wanted a repeat of that embrace, I knew better than to tempt either one of us any further. "Duty calls. Looks like I won't be able to go on that trip with you and Blair yet."

"Unlike yon fae prince, I'm in no rush. Just say the word." He grinned at me and trailed a finger down my cheek, leaving heat in its wake, which was pretty weird considering he was a sea-based entity. "I may not trust myself alone with you, but I'll take any chance to be together when we've got other parties along to keep us honest."

I grabbed that finger and gave it a squeeze, barely resisting kissing his knuckles because that would have been a little too retro weird. "You don't think absence would make the heart grow fonder?"

"It's not my heart that I'm worried about." Uh...did he mean... "It's yours, lad." Okay, so his mind wasn't in the gutter along with mine. "I want you to be sure, for your sake as well as mine." This time, his smile was crooked. "I'd rather not be tossed aside like a day-old catch again, and I want you to be certain it's not just selkie magnetism that's snared you." Lachlan must not be worried about retro weirdness because he lifted my hand, still clutching his finger, and kissed it like every Regency hero ever.

I didn't swoon, but it was a near thing.

CHAPTER FOUR

I bypassed the lobby, where I could hear Zeke's soothing tones as he responded to an unidentified person, Jordan piping up intermittently. Eleri awaited me outside Niall's office.

She jerked her head at the closed oak door with its intricate acorn and oak leaf carving. "Any idea what this is about?"

"Unfortunately," I said gloomily.

"Uh oh." She bit her lip. "Should I be worried about my job?"

"I'm probably more at risk. I'm the one on probation." Not to mention human. Even though Niall and Mal were cool with having a human in their midst, not everyone in the supe community was as tolerant. If Grizel demanded it, would Niall agree to fire me and let the council wipe my memory? I shook my hands to force blood into my fingers. I'd dreamed of magic and wonder all my life. Discovering it was real was more than I had ever hoped for, even though, by definition, I'd be a perpetual outsider.

To have that taken away after so short a time? To be shunted back to those days when I'd hoped and searched and *wanted*? Well, I'd put up with whatever punishment Niall decreed if it meant I didn't have to return to that life.

"Standing out here won't make things any easier," she said and knocked.

"No," I replied as Niall called, "Come in." But I could live in denial for a few more minutes, especially if they were among the last I'd experience with my knowledge intact.

We entered to find Niall leaning against his enormous oak desk—the leaf-and-acorn motif wasn't restricted to the door—with his arms crossed and a scowl that didn't make him less ridiculously handsome.

"You asked to see us, Your Highness?" Eleri chirped.

"Enough with the Your Highness shite," Niall growled. "You know that's not my life."

"Right." I cleared my throat. "I'm guessing this is about our excursion into Faerie?"

He sighed and pinched the bridge of his nose. "Do you have any idea how uncomfortable it is to face my brother when he has to deliver an official reprimand to me regarding the actions of my staff?"

"I'm guessing it's no picnic," I said.

"No," he replied and sighed again. "An official harassment complaint has been lodged with the King, and as such cannot be ignored."

Grizel hadn't struck me as someone who went in for bureaucratic intervention—she seemed more a hands-on kind of person—but she did say she was able to protect herself. Maybe this was another way to ensure we left her the hell alone.

"Do we need to offer an apology?" Eleri asked. "Because we don't have any problem with that."

Niall lifted an eyebrow—which didn't have nearly the effect on me that Lachlan's did. Must be the scar. Or maybe it was just Lachlan. "The complaint was not lodged against you, Eleri. Only against Hugh."

"What?" she squawked, and I was warmed a little by her indignation on my behalf. "But we were both there. In fact, we weren't the only—"

"I understand," I said, breaking in smoothly before she could implicate Jordan. To her credit, she got it immediately and clammed up. "Eleri's fae. She had a right to be there."

Niall grimaced. "That's pretty much the gist. But, Hugh. *Matt.*" I winced. Nobody at Quest ever called me by my real name unless they were trying to A) ground me or B) keep me from doing something stupid. In this case, it was probably both. "As a human, venturing into Faerie without either an FTA driver or an escort—"

"He had an escort!" Eleri said. "I was with him."

"An escort of *rank,*" Niall continued, emphasizing the word, "is incredibly dangerous. Yes, my brother and sister-in-law have instituted a number of progressive policies, but while most fae are happy about the changes, not all are. Change is difficult for fae. Some of them may never embrace the new order. So you need to be careful."

I swallowed nervously, remembering Grizel's avaricious glee and Lachlan's warning. "I will. I promise."

"I'm afraid your promise won't be enough." He swiveled and picked up a sheet of parchment, its edges curled as if it had been recently rolled up. "This is the official document recording the transgression and spelling out the conditions of your continuing engagement with the supernatural community."

"More probation?" That was probably the best I could hope for and was a long way from being the worst.

"At least another year," Niall said apologetically. "And regular check-ins with a designated official, where you'll need to supply a log of your interactions with supes and submit your camera for regular review."

"That's not fair," Eleri said. "It's not as though he was gallivanting around on his own or threatening the Secrecy Pact."

"Yes, well…" Niall rubbed the back of his neck. "Apparently, his association with you is doing him no favors either. Your clan chief considers you—" He glanced down at the parchment. "—

'disruptive, disrespectful, and disobedient, clearly an unchancy influence.'"

"Oh." She shrugged. "Can't argue with that."

"Is that all?" I asked.

"You're also to restrict your Faerie incursions to the regular FTA routes and are never to venture in without a registered driver unless you're in company with Mal or me."

"Fine," I said. It wasn't the greatest outcome—a probation officer? Seriously? But at least I still had a job and my memory.

"Oh, and Hugh?" Niall's expression managed to be stern and apologetic at the same time. "I'm sorry, but you're back on surveillance again."

Well, crap.

Niall signaled for us to go, and as we trudged down the hallway toward the lobby, Eleri patted my shoulder. "This totally isn't fair, kiddo. We can appeal. I'm sure if we explain—"

"Explain what? Appeal to whom? This came down from the King himself. There's not exactly a higher court, you know?" I smiled at her tightly. "Besides, I knew what we were doing was skirting the edge of allowable. You did too."

"Yeah, but I don't give a shit. I skirt the edge all the time."

"You're fae, though. You get a pass. I don't."

"Hugh." She grabbed my elbow and turned me to face her. "You're not *less* because you're human. In fact, compared to some of the asshole supes I've had to deal with—including my root-bound clan chief—you're so much *more* it's not even funny." Her smile was sly. "Lachlan certainly agrees with me."

"Shut up," I said, giddiness warring with the desolation in my middle. "You know we can't do anything about that until Wyn shows up to complete the sundering ceremony and sever their handfasting knot."

Her expression turned fierce. "We'll find him. Somehow, we'll figure out where he's hiding before you have to apply for Medicare."

"Oh thanks," I said dryly. "That's very comforting."

"You know what I mean." She let go of me and marched toward the lobby. "In fact, when I get home, I'm..." She stumbled to a halt at the end of the hall, her eyes widening as she stared into the lobby. "Human," she murmured.

I snorted. "Ho ho ho. Very funny. I'm the only one of those around here."

"No. That's what I mean." She jabbed a finger toward the lobby in the direction of Zeke's desk, although I couldn't see it from my position. "You're not. There's a human in the lobby right now, arguing with Zeke."

"That's impossible." For one thing, Zeke never argued. For another... "The security spells prevent any human but me from entering." I paused. But hadn't they allowed Blair in earlier? Maybe there was something wrong with the spells.

I peered around the doorjamb. Sure enough, there was a guy who looked as ordinary as me, glaring down at Zeke. He was wearing some kind of uniform—navy pants, a blue and white striped shirt with a name badge sewn on the pocket, a blue ball cap with some company logo on it that I didn't recognize.

"Sir," Zeke said, "I'm afraid there's a misunderstanding."

"No misunderstanding." The guy brandished his cell phone. "The map led me right to your door. GPS doesn't lie!"

"Aw," Eleri murmured at my shoulder, "that's so sweet. He believes in the omnipotence of technology."

"If you hadn't kept ignoring my phone calls," the guy continued, "I wouldn't have had to take the time to come down here. I've got a schedule to keep, you know. Other deliveries. Other restaurants. If you people would just do your job, I wouldn't have had to go to this trouble." Despite his confrontational words, the guy seemed frazzled rather than angry.

I glanced over my shoulder. We'd closed Niall's door on our way out. Should I let him know Zeke was being harassed by an unscheduled human?

"Oh, what app do you use for that?" Jordan chirped as he pulled out his own cell phone. "The FTA is really a lot more—"

"Hello!" I said almost desperately, striding into the lobby and subtly (I hoped) shouldering Jordan aside. "I'm Hugh. What seems to be the problem"—I glanced at his name badge—"Bob?"

From the corner of my eye, I caught Eleri shepherding Jordan down the hall, thank goodness. If I knew her, she'd stow him in Mal's empty office and give Niall the warning that we'd been invaded. But in the meantime, it was probably up to me as the, er, human interface and universal translator to take this guy's statement and usher him out. We'd figure out the problem with the security spells later.

"The *problem*," Bob said, "is that I pay my taxes for services that the government isn't providing. What good is animal control if you don't control animals?"

"Actually," Zeke said timidly, "we're not—"

"Why don't you tell me about the animal who's in need of control?" I said, gesturing Bob to the far side of the lobby. "Have a seat."

He peered at me suspiciously, but then huffed and stalked over to plop into a chair. Crap. I didn't have a notepad with me. But as I passed Zeke's desk, he smoothly handed me a legal pad and a pen, no doubt calling on his abilities to detect a person's true desire.

Demon office managers are the best.

I sat in the chair catercorner from Bob and crossed my legs, settling the pad on my knee and meeting his eyes with what I hoped was professional interest. "Can you describe the...er... encounter?"

"Encoun*ters*," he said. "Since nobody here bothered to respond to my previous calls."

"I'm very sorry about that." I shrugged apologetically. "Bureaucracy. You know how it is. But I'm listening now, and I promise we'll get the matter taken care of." Of course, how we intended to take care of it—keeping unsanctioned humans out of the office and off our phone—was probably not what Bob was hoping for. What can I say? Secrecy Pact.

"First time it happened was maybe...three days ago? I was making my usual delivery at the Burgerville on Cornell in Hillsboro when I saw it."

"Saw it? What exactly did you see?"

Bob swallowed, and it was clear that whatever he'd seen had spooked him badly. But then, people got spooked by different things. Jordan, for instance, had that serious aversion to water. Also logic, but then he was still a junior werewolf. None of them had a lot of sense.

"A dog."

"A dog," I repeated, nonplussed.

"Yeah. It was pawing at the dumpster."

I glanced at Zeke, who was watching us, eyes wide behind the bespelled glasses that let him see in Upper World light. "So a stray dog was nosing at the garbage. That seems pretty ordinar—"

"No, he was *pawing* at it. Like *bam bam bam*. And the dumpster was *rocking*."

I blinked. Okay, that was unusual. "Could you describe the dog, please?"

"Big. Like really big." He gulped, his prominent Adam's bobbing. "Taller than a Great Dane. White, or maybe cream. I'm not sure since it was before dawn and the parking lot lights weren't all that bright." He rubbed his palms on his trousers. "Like a ghost, you know?"

"A ghost dog who could rock a dumpster?"

He glared at me. "I know it sounds like I've gone off the deep end, but it was there, I tell you. And its eyes." He widened his, nearly bugging them out. "Glowing. Literally glowing like fire."

"Many animals' eyes reflect the light in a way that makes them look like they're—"

"No. My headlights weren't on. They were *glowing*, I tell you. They…they cast *shadows*."

"Oookay," I said, writing it all down because if this guy was seeing giant spectral hounds like something out of Conan Doyle cosplay, then we needed to humor him. "A ghost dog with glowing eyes who is powerful enough to displace a dumpster." I glanced up from my notes. "A full-sized dumpster?"

He nodded. "Yes. Packed to the brim, too, because it was trash collection day and the waste management truck doesn't show up until closer to noon."

I folded my hands on top of the pad, pen held loosely in my double fist. "Did the dog threaten you in any way? Growl? Try to bite you or… You said you were making deliveries to a Burgerville. Consumables?"

He nodded. "Beef for their burgers. All local stuff. High quality. They're known for that."

"I know." I smiled comfortingly. "For their seasonal specialties, too. Did the dog try to rush you for the meat?"

"No. Just stared at me with those eyes. Whined a little." Bob bridled a bit. "We've got strict safety protocols in place for delivery and receipt. Between me and the manager, we got everything inside safely." He adjusted his ball cap like it was his helmet of office. "And I made sure my truck was locked up tight beforehand too."

"Was the dog still there when you came out?"

Bob's shoulders slumped. "No. No sign of him when I drove out of the lot."

I nodded sympathetically. "I'm sorry no one could get out there to capture the dog when you sighted it. Since it disappeared, however, I'm not sure how we could locate it at the—"

"It was back the next day. And the one after that." He jerked his chin in a swift nod. "This morning too."

"I see." Well, this didn't seem to be much of an issue. I could notify actual animal control and have them take care of it. "It sounds like we just need to send an officer out to the Burgerville —"

Bob snorted. "Which one?"

I frowned at him. "I beg your pardon?"

"The damn thing showed up at every single one of the restaurants on my route—Hillsboro, Tigard, Beaverton. Even Newberg, on the other side of the Chehalem mountains."

The Chehalem hills weren't tall as far as Oregon mountain ranges went, but they were still a significant barrier. "Are you sure it was the same dog?"

He narrowed his eyes at me. "Not like I could mistake it. Have *you* ever seen a dog like that?"

"All right. You're sure. Was there a pattern? Did it appear in Hillsboro on Monday, for instance, and Tigard on Wednesday?"

He slapped his thighs. "You don't get it. It showed up at every one of those Burgervilles every day. Every time."

My frown deepened. "Are you saying that the dog could get from Hillsboro to Tigard as fast as you could drive? To Newberg too?"

"Yes!" He lifted his ball cap and swiped a hand across his forehead. "That's what I mean. It'd have to be a ghost dog to disappear and reappear like that, right?" It seemed like his forehead swipe was useless because sweat beaded along his hat band immediately. "And it's stalking me. I mean, why me? I'm just a meat delivery guy."

"Well, I expect most dogs would rather go for a burger than fries."

He scowled at me and rose to his feet. "This isn't a joke. This is affecting my job. It could affect the restaurants too. What if the dog shows up when customers are there? What if it goes for one of them? A kid? You guys need to do your damn job and keep us safe!"

"You're right. I apologize." I stood to face him. "If you could give me your route schedule, someone will trace it and see if they can pick up the dog's trail."

"Make sure they've got those whatchamacallems, spirit scanners, because they'll need it."

"Hugh," Zeke said softly.

I glanced over at him to see he'd slid a Quest business card across the desk. The number under our logo was my personal cell phone, not the Quest line. Message received. "Thanks, Zeke." I handed Bob the card. "Give me a call if you spot the dog again before the officer is able to apprehend it."

He snatched the card. "They won't. I'm telling you. That dog's a fricking ghost."

CHAPTER FIVE

When I got back upstairs from escorting Bob downstairs, Zeke was on the phone again, the handset held to his ear.

"Hello? Hello? Is anybody there?" He huffed an exasperated breath. "Hel*lo*?" Then he did something I'd never seen Zeke do before—he had a little temper tantrum, slamming the handset down with enough force to make Jordan, who was perched on a stool next to the desk where he could observe, inhale on a bite of scone. He coughed wildly, sending crumbs scattering across Zeke's desk, the phone—and my jeans.

"Sorry! Sorry!" he said, brushing at the mess on the desk, only succeeding in relocating everything to the carpet.

"Well, that was interesting." I collapsed back onto the chair I'd recently vacated. "Not Jordan's scone aspiration. Bob's little hallucinatory adventure."

Eleri plopped down in Bob's former seat and nudged one of my trainers with her boot. "What makes you think he was hallucinating?"

"Oh, come on. A giant spectral hound stalking Portland area Burgervilles? How likely is that?"

She lifted an eyebrow. "Let's see." She pointed at Zeke. "Demon." Herself. "Dryad." Jordan. "Doofus."

"Hey!" Jordan protested.

"My point," she said, "is that you more than anybody know that a giant spectral hound isn't just a story for house cat mamas to scare unruly kittens with."

I sighed. She had a point. Back in my tabloid photography days, I would have *killed* for a tip like this, especially if it panned out. So few of those tips ever did. In fact, it was only Ted's anonymous calls that resulted in shots of actual cryptids—the cryptid in question being Ted himself in partial shift. I scratched the back of my head. I had vague memories of another tip that paid off—something involving a cave and a flash and maybe... Nah, it was gone again. Must be a dream—or a hallucination to rival Bob's.

"I'll call real animal control," I said. "If they don't—"

The phone rang again. Zeke glared at it with the loathing he usually reserved for his former demon supervisor. The phone console was lucky he didn't have a Louisville Slugger handy.

"I'll get it!" Jordan piped. "I could use the practice."

Zeke gave Jordan an open-palmed *be my guest* gesture. You never had to ask Jordan twice.

"Hellllooo!" he caroled, a wide grin on his face. "You don't say.... Really? That's amazing. Uh huh. Uh huh. Right. Thank you for calling!" He hung up and beamed at us.

"So..." Eleri said. "Who was it?"

"Oh, there was nobody there," he said cheerfully.

I shared a WTH glance with Zeke and Eleri. "So you just had a conversation with a dead line?"

Jordan shuddered. "Ugh. Don't say dead."

"Jordan," I said warningly.

He gave me an earnest look, complete with puppy eyes. "I need to work on my humaning skills. You guys are always telling me that, right?"

"Yes," Zeke said slowly, obviously waiting for the other Jordan-shoe to drop.

"So what better way to practice than on calls with nobody on the other end? I can't screw up that way and Zeke doesn't have to keep answering prank calls." His eyebrows drew together in a disgruntled frown. "I still think it's my old pack mates." His eyes popped wide and he blinked rapidly. "Not the other guys at the Dog House—I mean the Howling Residence. They'd never do that. But a couple of my cousins are kind of...well... jerks. They've been..."

"Bullying you?" Eleri asked gently.

"They call it *teasing*," Jordan said with a catch in his voice, "but they can be pretty mean sometimes."

"Jordan," I said. "If they're really bullying you—"

"Oh, I can ignore them now since I'm living up here at the Dog House and they're back at the pack compound in Jackson County. And now that the rules are changing and we don't *have* to go back to our original pack after our Howling, they can't bother me anymore." He frowned at the phone. "Although I wish they'd stop bugging Zeke."

Zeke smiled at Jordan and patted him on the shoulder. "I appreciate your concern. But it's all right. Like you, my life is so much better than it used to be that I have no room for complaints." He put his headset back on. "But thank you for that reminder, Jordan. I should never take my good fortune for granted and let my temper get the better of me."

I stood up. "I'll call Washington County Animal Control and let them know—"

"No."

All of us started at Niall's deep voice from the hallway. Jeez, how long had he been standing there? He strode into the lobby, a thoughtful expression on his face. "This isn't a job for humans. Not if that man—"

"Bob," Eleri said helpfully.

Niall inclined his head. "Thank you. Not if Bob could walk unhindered into the office, let alone complete multiple calls."

I leaned forward, propping my elbows on my knees. "Yeah, I wanted to talk to you about that. I think something must be wonky with our security spells. Earlier, Lachlan brought a human kid in with him. And then there's Bob and his giant spectral hound report. Aren't the spells supposed to keep humans out?" Eleri choked on a laugh and I glared at her. "Other than me, I mean."

Niall perched on the edge of Zeke's desk. For a prince, he was pretty dang informal most of the time. "You're looking at the spells from the wrong direction. They're not exclusionary. They're *inc*lusionary."

Jordan goggled at him. "Huh?"

"They're not intended to keep anybody in particular out," Niall said, "they're configured to allow anybody in—either physically or with any of our communication options—who has legitimate business with the supernatural community."

"So you think," I said slowly, "that there really *is* a giant spectral hound?"

Niall sighed, annoyance briefly marring his perfect features. "It could be an apparition conjured up by a mage. An air elemental, perhaps, although their manifestations aren't generally corporeal enough to rock a dumpster with an appendage."

"It's not really a...a ghost, is it?" Jordan's voice dropped to a whisper on the last words.

Niall smiled down at him fondly. "Given that the only known necromancer is not only stripped of power but incarcerated, no. None of the other elemental mages traffic in death."

"Demons could, though," Zeke said. "Sheol is basically full of the souls of nonliving persons."

"Persons," Niall said. "Not dogs."

Zeke gazed into the air for an instant, obviously thinking. "No. Not dogs. I thought I saw a honey badger once, but it was probably just Ukobach in a bad mood."

Niall fixed his dark, intense gaze on me. "Bob shouldn't have been able to contact us, and yet he did. I think it's worth checking out before we get the human authorities involved, and since you're once more available for surveillance duty, Hugh..."

I groaned inwardly, although I made myself smile in agreement. Staking out fast-food restaurants in the wee hours of the morning wasn't exactly my dream assignment, but then I had nobody to blame but myself. Was I really so desperate for affection that I'd jeopardize my job for my heart?

Short answer: Yes. Longer and more logical answer: No, because I still didn't know whether this thing between Lachlan and me would go anywhere (or if it wasn't anything other than selkie magnetism) and it couldn't last anyway because I'd age and he wouldn't and besides he was still married and who *knew* when his nearly ex-husband would become his actual ex-husband.

Which brought me back to the short answer again and the reason I'd screwed up in the first place. Yeah, whether I was Matt Steinitz or Hugh Mann, my middle name was Desperation.

Unless it was Stupid, which was also a distinct possibility.

"Okay," I said, aiming for a little professionalism if not enthusiasm. "I'll call Bob and get his delivery schedule—"

"No," Niall said. "We can't depend on that, since there's no evidence that the dog *only* appears during his deliveries. The only restaurant that matters is the first one on his route, which we already know. Stake it out, starting just before the restaurant closes tonight. Then you'll be able to determine whether the animal—"

"*Alleged* animal," Eleri offered with a smirk.

Niall shot her a quelling glance, not that it affected her much. "Whether it seems to be following the truck." But then he winked. "Or whether it's just got a ghostly hankering for a Vampire Slayer burger."

Jordan's mouth dropped open. "They have those?" He glanced around and lowered his voice to a rough whisper. "Does Mr. Moreau know?"

"It's just a burger prepared with a lot of different garlicky ingredients," I told him. "One of their seasonal offerings. And since vampires aren't really affected by garlic, you don't need to worry about Casimir. But you," I narrowed my eyes at Niall, "are enjoying this way too much."

He sighed. "I'm not. Really, I'm not. But as unlikely as it is that this case affects the supe community, ignoring it now that the spells have allowed Bob to cross our threshold would definitely affect us."

My throat got tight over his use of *us*. And before you point it out, I'm well aware that although Niall said *us* in a way that seemed to include me, that didn't make me belong to the supe community. I was still just an inconvenient appendage, not too many notches above supe groupie. But I was part of Quest Investigations, and that made a difference. I needed to put my love life on the back burner and focus on my job.

Niall gripped my shoulder. "Look at it this way, boyo. The sooner we rebuild the trust between you and the council, the sooner you'll be able to return to...shall we say, more interesting cases?"

I nodded. "Right. Surveillance it is." Except... "Crap. I broke my telephoto lens during that dryad case." I glanced at Eleri, who was present at the Great Dryad Debacle, but she was studying her fingernails, not looking at me. Avoidance much? "I haven't had a chance to replace it yet."

And it wasn't only because I'd been too focused on Lachlan, either. I thought I was done with surveillance jobs and that I'd have a chance to find the perfect lens. Because the council had insisted that my camera be ensorcelled so I couldn't release any damning photos to the human press, it took a special kind of lens to withstand the spells without melting.

I'd lost more lenses that way.

"I can research replacements for you if you like, Hugh," Zeke said. The phone rang again and he winced.

I chuckled. "Don't worry about it. Now that I think of it, it's not like I'll need it on this job. The restaurants generally have small footprints and parking lots. And it's not as though it'll matter if the dog spots me." I cleared my throat and stared at Eleri. "Unlike the fallout from a certain tree of heaven stakeout."

"Oh, shut up," she said. "You startled us, that's all. It was a tree that broke the lens anyway, not one of us."

"Did you keep harassing me afterward because you were startled too?" I asked dryly. Eleri and her "book club" had never passed up a chance to give me plant-based grief.

"Of course not," she said with a grin. "We only did that because it was fun."

CHAPTER
SIX

That night was chilly—it was mid-October after all—but clear, something you couldn't always count on in Oregon at this time of year. I arrived at the Hillsboro Burgerville about half an hour before closing to check in with the manager and let her know what I was doing. She didn't seem surprised—apparently Bob had shared his close encounter of the canine kind with her.

The restaurant was located in the parking lot of a strip mall across from the Hillsboro Airport. Its rear door and private dumpster were concealed inside a tiny brick-walled enclosure, the better to provide a pleasant experience for their diners. Unfortunately, the dumpsters used by the other merchants weren't nearly as unobtrusive. In fact, they were downright revolting—gray, battered, and overfull—and located right next to the Burgerville's drive-through lane.

I couldn't imagine a giant spectral hound with even a smidge of self-respect rocking those nasty things, so I set my camp stool up beside my beater Honda at the edge of the lot across from the airfield. I had a partially obstructed view of the private courtyard, but I wasn't close enough to spook any ghostly pooch who might show up for a snack or a dumpster percussion session.

I draped the strap of my Nikon over my neck, frowning at the wide-angle lens. Not my first choice, because it exaggerated perspective a little too much, but as I'd told Niall, the target area wasn't that far away and it wasn't as if we'd need to identify someone's face or relative size in a lineup.

The four legs and tail should clinch that, no problem.

The traffic along Cornell and 25th was already light, only the occasional headlights sweeping the parking lot and where I huddled in the relative shelter of my car. If things stayed slow—and what were the odds they wouldn't?—I could retreat inside it to warm up periodically as the temperature dropped overnight. It wasn't supposed to hit freezing, but mid-forties was cold enough to make me wish for heated underwear.

Speaking of heated underwear...

The phone in my jacket pocket vibrated against my hip, and when I pulled it out to check, the message was from Lachlan. He and Blair must have gone out on his boat anyway—I tried not to feel forlorn or resentful that they'd gone without me, because Blair deserved a little fun in their life and Lachlan wasn't attached to me at the hip.

Unfortunately.

I chuckled softly because he'd sent me a picture of Blair holding a fish of some kind—I probably needed to brush up on my fish species if I was going to be dating a selkie, especially a selkie who ran chartered fishing cruises. The kid's face was screwed up in an obvious *ewww* and they were holding the fish as far away from their body as possible.

The ellipsis bubble appeared while I was still laughing.

Lachlan: Blair's first catch.

Me: Tell the truth—did Blair catch it, or did you?

Lachlan: Their hook, their fish. I helped land it, though.

Me: Looks like they'd rather throw it back.

Lachlan: [laugh emoji] At first. Changed their mind when we grilled it for dinner though.

Me: [smile emoji] Glad you both had a good day.

Lachlan: Wish you'd been with us. Next time.

Me: Yeah. Next time.

I drew a shaky breath, wondering if *next time* would be any different. Or if *next time* would be *last time* because Lachlan would realize how incompatible our lives were. I resolutely tucked my phone back in my pocket before I succumbed to the temptation for more flirty texting.

It was foolish to get more involved with Lachlan while he was still technically unavailable, because that would be wrong. But hey, I'm human—which is totally part of the problem, right? —so I couldn't resist the flirting, the heated glances, the occasional touch, even if the unresolved sexual tension was about to make my head explode.

No, not *that* head. Jeez, minds out of the gutter, okay? Bad enough that my own spends half its time there lately.

As I sat in the lee of the Honda, I started to wonder whether this whole situation—the appearance of an alleged supernatural animal, a human being able to breach our security, the endless phone calls that had continued to plague Zeke all day—might be something more sinister.

And by that, I don't mean an actual ghost dog. But when I'd discovered undeniable existence of the supe community by way of Ted's incubus husband's twelve-foot black wingspan, I hadn't been the only human in the tribunal's crosshairs. The asshole who'd threatened supe children—*children*, for Pete's sake—had been human too, even though the person who'd been paying him was a renegade angel.

What if he'd shared those shots with somebody else before the council clamped him down? I wasn't selling photos to the tabloids anymore, but what if somebody else was? All it needed was one grainy snapshot to go viral to focus unwanted attention on the supernatural folk living in more or less plain sight among humans.

I leaned over to grab my travel mug, thoughtfully loaded with our stellar office coffee by Zeke, who'd also packed me an entire day pack full of snacks. I was debating whether to make inroads on those—the aroma of grilling burgers was impossible to ignore so close to the restaurant, even if the place was mere minutes away from closing—when I heard a rattle from the other side of the public dumpsters.

Crap, I'd made the wrong assumption—the giant spectral hound didn't have any self-respect after all.

I let go of the mug and it tipped, rolling under the Honda in a wink of stainless steel. *Dammit.* I'd retrieve it later and hope it hadn't spilled all over the tarmac. For now, I crouched by the bumper, my camera at the ready. It was probably nothing more than an employee from one of the other businesses cleaning up at the end of their shift. I'd missed out on money shots before by not being ready, though, and I wasn't about to do it again. Not now, not when success might mean exposing a threat to the supe community that I'd come to love so much—even if most of them didn't feel a similar affection for me.

Another rattle. A thump. And—

"Sorry! Sorry, Hugh!"

Oh, for crying out loud. "Jordan?"

Jordan peeked around the corner of the nasty dumpster. "Um, hi?"

"There's no point in hiding now. He's seen you." Eleri's tone was laced with a combination of amusement and resignation.

I straightened up as they skirted the overflowing bins and headed toward me. "What are you two doing here?"

Jordan held up a Burgerville bag. "Sweet potato fries!"

Eleri shook her head with a wry smile. "The sweet potato fries were a bonus. We, um…" She looked down at her Doc Martens. "The mess with Grizel was just as much our faults as yours."

"Don't try to shift the blame," I said, taking a fry from the bag Jordan held out to me. "It was my plan, and it wasn't well thought out. Niall was right to reprimand me. You guys were just being good friends, helping me out."

Jordan beamed. "See? I told you he wouldn't be mad, Eleri. I've helped Hugh on cases before."

"How*ever*," I said, spearing him with a narrow-eyed glance, "unexpected 'help' can derail an entire plan. So, Jordan? Next time you want to assist, *ask* first."

"Yeah." Eleri nudged him with her elbow. "And if the answer is no—like, oh, when I told you not to buy an entire bushel of sweet potato fries—you need to let it go."

I took another fry. "Hey, no complaints about these. But Eleri's right. Aren't you junior weres supposed to work on impulse control during your Howling?"

He sighed and munched on three fries at once. "Yeah. But it's hard to know what's going to happen until it *happens*, you know? How can you consider your actions if you don't know what action the action will—"

"Don't move," Eleri said, her voice low and fierce.

"What?" Jordan said. "Why?"

"Be *quiet*," she growled, and by some miracle, Jordan obeyed.

She jerked her head toward the brick enclosure and mouthed, *Dog*.

I lifted my camera, ready to capture the marauding Great Dane or Great Pyr or whatever large mixed breed had gotten Bob's knickers in a knot. But when I spotted the animal, its head down while it nosed the base of the Burgerville dumpster, my mouth dropped open.

Because *holy crap*. It actually *was* a giant spectral hound.

Well, giant, yes. It probably stood at least as high as my waist. I'm not super tall—five eleven—but that was still one big dog. A big and clearly corporeal dog, because although its white coat almost gleamed in the uncertain parking lot light, it was clearly solid, its ears dark.

Next to me, Jordan made a strangled *Nngh,* and the dog raised its head.

Double holy crap. Bob hadn't been blowing smoke out his ass, because he was right—the dog's eyes glowed amber, bright enough to illuminate the small courtyard and throw a spear of light into the parking lot.

"What the hell is *that*?" I murmured.

"*Cwn Annwn*," Eleri said, and even though her voice was barely audible, it held both awe and fear.

"*Cwn*— What? You mean it's one of Herne the Hunter's pack?"

She nodded as the dog took a couple of hesitant steps toward us. "Definitely. A young one, though. Still mostly a puppy?"

"You mean it'll get *bigger*?" I squeaked, which caused the dog's ears to perk up. *Uh oh.* The *Cwn Annwn* were only supposed to hunt traitors, conspirators, and oath-breakers, but exactly how precise could a lone dog's perceptions be? Would it consider my lapse in judgment to be the equivalent of breaking an oath?

"Maybe not taller, but it'll fill out." Eleri squinted at the hound. "Look. You can see its ribs. No wonder it's staking out the Burgervilles. It's starving."

"Starving?" Jordan said. "That's not good. Dogs shouldn't starve." He pulled a fry out of the bag and waggled it in front of him, taking a couple of steps toward the dog. "Here, boy."

"Jordan," I hissed, "what did we just say about considering your actions?" The dog crept closer, and I hoped that laser-beam gaze was focused on the fry and not Jordan's entire hand. "How do you know it's a boy, anyway?"

He glanced over his shoulder at me. "From his scent, of course. He—*yikes!*" The dog lunged forward and snatched the fry out of Jordan's fingers, downing it in one gulp. His eyes seemed to glow brighter, and he whined low in his throat.

"He's, ah, not going to, you know, *track* us, is he?" I asked Eleri, unnerved by the intense way the dog stared at Jordan. Or rather, at Jordan's bag of sweet potato fries.

"One this young?" She gave her head a tiny shake, obviously not trying to draw the beast's attention. "I doubt he's run with the pack at all yet, although he might this Calan Gaeaf."

Jordan dug in his bag and offered the dog another fry, which he took almost delicately. "Who's a good boy, then?" he crooned.

Oh, brother. All we needed was for Jordan to bond with a traitor-tracking hound. That could not possibly end well. "What's he doing here? I mean, shouldn't he be in Faerie with Herne and the rest of the pack?"

"Herne doesn't actually live in Faerie."

"So where does he live?"

She shrugged. "Nobody knows. He comes out for the Wild Hunt on Calan Gaeaf and Calan Mai"—I translated: While Calan Gaeaf was the equivalent of Samhain/Halloween, Calan Mai equaled Beltane or May Day, more or less—"and when someone blows the horn to summon him."

"Great," I grumbled. "Then how are we supposed to return his dog to him?"

"Oh, the pack doesn't live with Herne. They're housed in the kennels in Faerie, tended by a kennel master, a bauchan whose family has been in charge of caring for them since the beginning."

I studied the dog, who was accepting fry after fry from Jordan with what seemed extremely good manners for an animal who was clearly hungry. "Why is he out here? He's obviously hurting for food. Why not go back to the kennels and get fed and"—I noticed some burrs stuck in the thick white fur —"groomed?"

"If it meant dinner, I'd always go home," Jordan said, patting the dog's head as he wolfed down another fry. "So if he's scrounging around here instead of going back?" Jordan looked at us and shrugged. "Maybe he can't."

CHAPTER
SEVEN

I froze, my breath stalling in my chest. "Holy crap, Eleri," I croaked. "Do you think *we* let him out? After the run-in with Grizel?" I had been more concerned with licking my own wounds and keeping Jordan's naughty bits covered than whether we were being followed by anyone two- or four-legged. If it was my fault this poor dog was homeless and starving, I deserved permanent surveillance duty. Or worse.

She met my gaze, her eyes wide and lips parted, but then shook her head. "No. Bob said the first sighting was three days ago, and we didn't confront Grizel until this morning. Time in Faerie runs at a different pace than here in the Outer World, but it doesn't run *backwards*."

I breathed a little easier. "So somehow he got stuck out here?"

She edged closer to the dog, who was still scarfing down fries. She didn't touch him, but she studied his fur and paws. "I don't think he's stuck necessarily. Remember, Bob said he showed up at every one of the delivery sites on the same day. There's only one way he could manage that."

"He took a shortcut through Faerie," I said.

"Exactly. And check his paws." She pointed at the beast's feet, which were the size of dinner plates. "No sign of wear or injury, so he's not been pounding the Outer World pavement, despite the mileage he's covered."

"So if he can get back into Faerie, why not stay there? Go home and join the rest of his pack and score a square meal or three?"

As the dog was chowing down on his latest fry, Jordan reached out and scratched behind his giant ear, which wasn't black as I'd originally thought—it was red. "Maybe his pack wasn't nice to him. That happens with wolves, so it might happen with the coo— coon-whatever dogs too."

Eleri rested her hand on the dog's back. "What is it, *ci dwp*? Why can't you go home?" The dog lifted an expressive tufted eyebrow and gave Eleri the side-eye, but kept his main focus on Jordan's apparently bottomless bag of sweet potato fries.

I gave her a side-eye of my own when she didn't say anything else. "Well?"

She tore her attention away from teasing a burr out of the dog's fur with fingers gone decidedly twiggy. "Well what?"

"What did he say?"

She awarded me a disgusted glance. "Probably something along the lines of *Keep those fries coming and I won't savage you.*"

"He wouldn't savage anybody," Jordan protested. "Would you, Doop?

Eleri barked—heh—a laugh. "*What* did you call him?"

Jordan looked at her as he dug into the bag, the dog nearly vibrating with impatience. "Doop. That's what you called him." His brows puckered under his floppy brown hair. "There was another word too, but I missed it. I figured he'd told you his name."

"First," she said, her tone implying that both Jordan and I needed a swift kick in the pants, "what gave either of you the idea that I could converse with animals?"

I blinked at her. "You talk to trees."

"Yes," she said, "because they're *trees*. I'm a *dryad.*"

I shared a glance with Jordan. "Did you know that?" He shook his head, so it wasn't just the human who was clueless in this situation.

"Second," she said, "I called him *ci dwp*."

Jordan snapped his fingers. "That was the other word! Kee!"

"*Ci dwp* means *stupid dog* in Welsh. So when you call him Doop—"

"I called him stupid?" Jordan's face fell. He turned back to the dog and offered him three fries. "I'm so sorry."

"Don't be," Eleri said. "Considering his recent behavior, it's pretty à propos." She sighed. "The question is, what do we do now?"

I don't know about you, but the answer was pretty clear to me. "We take him home. To Faerie."

Eleri bit her lip, eyeing the dog with obvious misgiving. "All right. Although dryads and dogs don't have the most traditionally *collegial* relationship." She glared at Jordan. "The whole peeing against trees thing tends to be an issue, particularly if we're bonded with the tree in question."

"Sorry." Jordan had the grace to look both embarrassed and apologetic. He'd used that particular tactic in one of my prior cases and it hadn't worked out especially well—in fact, that had been when my telephoto lens had gotten lunched by a flailing tree.

"I've lost more shoes that way," she muttered, "but needs must. Come on, *ci dwp*." She snapped her fingers at the dog—who, I suspected, was destined to be Doop forever. He ignored her. "Home. Faerie. Kennel. *Food*."

I smirked at her. "Looks like you should stick to talking to trees. They pay more attention."

"Shut up," she growled.

I studied the dog. He was approximately the size of a pony. Would he fit in the back seat of the Honda? Maybe, although it would be close. "It's my case. I need to take him back."

"But Hugh," Eleri said, "you can't. You're restricted to FTA routes only, *with* a driver."

I shrugged. "So? I'll call Frang." Doop might come up to my waist, but he'd only hit Frang slightly above the knee. "I just need to get the dog to an FTA stop."

"Oh, really?" Eleri crossed her arms. "The nearest FTA stop is in the wetlands over by Dr. MacLeod's place—"

"You mean *Mal's* place," Jordan said.

Jordan still had a bit of a hero-worship thing going with our other boss. While Eleri would never admit to hero worship, she definitely had a sincere admiration for Bryce MacLeod, Mal's husband, who was both druid and environmental sciences professor.

"Since they're married, the place belongs to both of them. But that's beside the point. I'll just load Doop into my car and take him over there. You guys don't need to get involved." I patted her arm. "I don't want to get you into any more trouble."

She *hmmmph*ed. "I'm way more likely to get *you* in trouble. Just ask my clan chief, so that argument won't fly."

"No, Eleri. I need to prove to the council that I'm able to abide by their decree, which includes following Niall's instructions. He asked me to handle this, to make certain the Secrecy Pact wasn't being threatened." I gestured to Doop, who was pawing the ground at Jordan's feet because the fries weren't appearing quickly enough. "What do you suppose will happen if I *don't* take him back? He'll either starve—"

"No!" Jordan looped an arm around Doop's neck. "We can't let him starve."

"—or he might resort to attacking a human in his desperation for food. Bob or one of the Burgerville employees, or maybe just some random kid munching a cookie on their way home from school."

The more I thought about it, the more I was convinced this was the perfect plan. Return the dog, earn the kennel master's gratitude, and prove myself capable of solving a case without chaos and destruction.

Win-win-win.

And as a bonus, Doop would get a better dinner than a steady diet of dumpster fare and werewolf handouts.

I strode to the back of the Honda and popped the trunk.

"You're not putting him in *there*?" Jordan said, scandalized.

"Yes, Jordan. I'm stuffing a dog the size of my living room sofa into the trunk of an '86 Civic." I grabbed the day pack and camp stool and slung them inside. "Of course not. But to fit him in the back seat, I can't have anything else there."

I crouched down and fished my errant travel mug out from under my car. It had landed with the sip opening down, so the coffee had all leaked out. *Dammit.* On the other hand, I didn't have an all-night surveillance gig ahead of me, so it hardly mattered.

I opened the back door. Luckily, I'd recently cleaned out the car, so the rear seat was clear. "Okay, Doop. In you go." He didn't move, although he gave me the doggy equivalent of a *Seriously?* glare. The glowing eyes added a definite Spielberg FX vibe. He lifted his—lip? Do dogs have lips?—and exposed a single fang.

Eleri chuckled. "I could be wrong, but I think he just turned down your offer. Somebody must have warned him about accepting rides from strange men."

"Very funny." I whistled and patted my leg, which earned me a barely audible growl. Okay, so he wasn't a fan of whistling. I propped my hands on my hips. "This isn't working."

Jordan took out what had to be the last sweet potato fry. He dove into the back seat, scooted all the way across, and patted the seat next to him. "Let's go, Doop. Eleri, you can have shotgun."

"Jordan," I began, "you can't—"

Doop lolloped over to the car and climbed inside, his rear paws scrabbling on the door frame.

"Apparently he can," Eleri said dryly, "when both of us can't."

I scrubbed my hands through my hair. "This is my problem. You guys shouldn't have to get involved."

She bumped my biceps with her fist. "We're volunteering, Hugh. That's what a team does." She opened her hand and gave my arm a tiny shake. "That's what *friends* do. Now..." She dusted off her palms. "I believe I've got shotgun." She darted to the other side of the car and climbed in.

I sighed and stowed my camera back in the bag. When I got behind the wheel, I handed the bag to Eleri. "Here. You can hold this." She accepted it with appropriate reverence. Eleri could be prickly—literally—but she knew how important my equipment was to me. She'd never risk it for the sake of snark.

I glanced in my rearview mirror and saw nothing but white fur. "You okay back there, Jordan?"

"Yes," he said, breathless, his voice maybe a little higher than usual, "but maybe drive fast? Doop is kinda heavy. And I think he might be sick, because he's cold. Like *really* cold."

"I'll do my best, but we really don't want to be pulled over." Because if human animal control got a gander at Doop, the Secrecy Pact would be well and truly screwed.

So while I didn't break any traffic laws, I didn't dawdle on the way, either. I slowed as I turned onto Mal's street. It was a cul-de-sac, the wetlands wrapping around three quarters of it. Mal and Bryce's house was at the apex. Mal's brother, Dr. Kendrick, and his husband, David Evans, lived next door. Since their yards abutted the wetlands, neither of their yards were fenced, although the ones on the other side of the cul-de-sac were.

I stopped a couple of houses down from the Evans-Kendricks. No lights were on inside, and the Kendrick-MacLeod place only had a faint glow coming from around its blinds. Since Mal and Bryce tended to get, er, enthusiastic about their private time together, I had no desire to interrupt.

I turned off the car and killed the headlights. "We'll cut down the side of Dr. Kendrick's place."

"Whatever you say." Eleri got out and shut the door as softly as my beater allowed—which wasn't very. She was still holding my camera bag, even without my asking her to. Yeah, my new BFF had learned *that* about me in our brief friendship: Regardless of the relative safety of any neighborhood, I didn't trust my camera to the Honda's dubious protection if I could help it.

I climbed out too, but after I shut my door, Jordan hadn't moved. Of course, the back seat was still overfull of the Welsh equivalent of hellhound, so he probably *couldn't* move. He'd been oddly silent—for Jordan—on the way over. Could he have suffocated under Doop's furry bulk?

I yanked open the door and Doop's tail immediately flopped out and began wagging, nearly taking out my kneecap. "Jordan? Are you okay?"

"Fine," he wheezed. "But I'd like to get out now."

I eyed Doop's doggy butt. "Eleri? Maybe open the door on your side?"

"I don't know," she said, although she opened the door. "Maybe Doop should just wear the car. It might be easier than extracting him."

Jordan's hand shot up above the roof on Eleri's side, the Burgerville bag in his hand. "Fry," he gasped, and it sounded as though his teeth were chattering. "Hurry."

Eleri snagged the sack and dug around in it. "Sheesh, Jordan, there's nothing left." I snapped my fingers. Eleri glared at me. "We've already determined that doesn't work."

"That's not what I— Oh, never mind." I popped the trunk so I could retrieve the day pack. Zeke had filled it with enough snacks for three people—hmmm, had he somehow known Eleri and Jordan would show up? Demon abilities were mysterious, but I didn't think foresight was one of Zeke's skills.

Maybe he just knew us all really well by now.

Aha! A turkey wrap. That ought to do the trick. I pulled it out and tossed the pack back. The sandwich was cut into two-inch slices, a decent mouthful for Doop. I unrolled the paper wrapper and teased one slice out.

When I closed the trunk, I choked on a laugh, because Doop's tail was protruding from one side of the Honda and his head from the other, exactly as if he were wearing the car as a full metal tutu—with bonus werewolf companion, because the back of Jordan's shaggy brown head was visible through the rear window.

I joined Eleri and held out the tidbit. "Come on, Doop. No more sweet potato fries, but we've got something just as good." The sandwich smelled amazing, in fact. If Doop didn't want it, I'd happily take it off his hands. Paws. Whatever.

Doop's nose quivered, and he emitted a whine that was more inquisitive than distressed. Amid a scrabble of paws and what seemed like twice the number of legs, with an accompanying *Ooof* from Jordan, the dog scrambled out of the car. I retreated several steps so there'd be room for him, glancing over my shoulder to make sure we weren't attracting any attention from the neighborhood residents.

By the time I turned back, Doop had snapped up the sandwich slice, his massive jaws working, and Jordan was climbing gingerly out of the car. I drew him up onto the sidewalk. "Are you okay?"

He smiled shakily through chattering teeth, his face pale under the yellowish gleam of the streetlights—although maybe that light was coming from Doop's eyes. "Yeah. It wasn't too bad. But his paw was right by my—" His eyes widened and next to us, Eleri snorted.

"Jordan?" I grabbed his arm, startled by how *cold* his jacket sleeve was. "What is it? What's wrong?"

Jordan gulped. "Doop is, um, sniffing my butt."

Somehow, I managed not to laugh. I'd lost count of the times Mal or Chase, Jordan's Howling RA, had warned him about butt sniffing. "Is it different when you're on the other side of the sniff?"

He sidestepped away from a disappointed-looking Doop. "Definitely."

"I think we may have found something the dog'll follow other than food," Eleri said, a laugh still buried in her voice.

"Then let's get on with it. Because after we've delivered Doop to the kennels? We're going for pie." I handed the rest of the turkey wrap to Jordan and took my camera bag from Eleri, looping the strap crosswise over my chest. "And guys?" I smiled at them both, hoping I infused my smile with all the gratitude I was feeling. "Thanks."

For a wonder, considering we were trooping across an open expanse of grass like some kind of weird low-budget parade, we made it to the edge of the wetlands with no trouble. I took the lead when we got to the berm surrounding what Bryce called a pond, but Mal insisted was a swamp. "Stay on the path and keep Doop out of the water. Bry— Dr. MacLeod is really particular about maintaining the environmental integrity here."

Jordan winced. "Don't worry. Nobody's getting wet if I can help it."

Jordan and water. It was a thing.

We skirted the edge of the pond, the cattails at its edge whispering in the breeze, until we passed the treeline. Here, safely hidden from any watchers, I pulled out the distinctive FTA voucher: an oak leaf embossed with a Celtic rune in gold. "Cludo Frang," I said. After the somewhat frantic end of our last case, Bryce had arranged with Niall's brother—King of Faerie—to alter the spell to include a specific driver request.

Frang, in all his mountainous glory, stepped out from between two birch trees. "Where to—*aieee!*"

I blinked. Had Frang just *squealed*? I glanced at Eleri, but she looked just as shocked as me. "Frang? You okay?"

"I didn't do it. Or if I did, I didn't mean to. I must have been drunk. I can never hold my fire mead. But I haven't had a drop since I started driving for the FTA." He dropped to his knees with a whimper. "Please don't hurt me."

"Frang." I took a step closer. "Seriously, dude, what's wrong?"

He pointed at Doop. "*C-Cwn Annwn.*"

Oh. Right. Doop was part of Herne's pack, tracker of traitors, scourge of oath breakers, doom of conspirators—although considering he was presently scarfing up another slice of turkey wrap, his ears pricked and his tail wagging, he wasn't at his most scourgelike or doom-laden at the moment.

"It's okay, Frang," I put a hand under his massive elbow to help him up. *Ooof.* I might as well try to lift the Honda. I settled for patting him on the shoulder. "He's not out with Herne. But he *is* the reason we called you. We need to return him to the kennels."

"The kennels," he said, the whites of his eyes showing. "The kennels where the entire *pack* of *Cwn Annwn* live?"

Eleri tilted her head. "Are there others?"

I elbowed her. Now was not the time to distract Frang. I had pie in my sights and I wanted this night to be done. "We just need to turn him over to the kennel master. Nothing more. I, uh, suppose you've heard that my access to Faerie is restricted?"

"*Temporarily* restricted," Eleri declared.

"Yeah. I'd heard." Frang's voice was still at least an octave above his usual basso profundo.

"So we need you. Unless you accompany us, we can't return Doop to the kennels." Doop snapped up the last slice of turkey roll. "Think of it as making the Outer World safe for convenience food." I smiled at him encouragingly. "Like doughnuts!" Frang was a, er, hound for the doughnuts from Wanda's Diner.

He sighed as he got heavily to his feet. "All right." He pointed a finger the size of a kielbasa at me. "But if that hound starts chasing me, you're on your own."

CHAPTER EIGHT

Despite Frang paying almost no attention to the path in front of him—he was too busy looking over his shoulder at Doop, who was prancing along happily at Jordan's side—we made it up the tor inside Faerie with no trouble.

"Kennels are in what used to be the common lands, Seelie and Unseelie." Frang snorted. "Now everything's common ground."

Eleri looked up at him curiously. "Does that bother you?"

He shrugged his enormous shoulders. "Nah. I was Unseelie, so the changes are all to the good. Don't have to worry about the king lopping off your head because he doesn't like his soup, or a band of Daoine Sidhe out for a spot of mayhem ambushing you on the way to the loo." He scratched the back of his head. "I hear tell that some of the Seelie aren't as happy though." He grinned down at me. "Not so special now that we're all on the same side, are they?" He paused, squinting at a fork in the trail. After a moment, he nodded. "Right. This way."

He led us down a path bordered by some kind of graceful, pale-barked trees that I didn't recognize, their branches laced above us to make a living tunnel. Eleri hummed in pleasure and I could swear that the trees hummed back. Then we stepped out onto a plateau with—

"Holy crap," I breathed. "The Stone Circle."

I'd heard of this place—like Stonehenge, if it was complete and about twice as big. The fae used it for important ceremonies. I gulped, because some of those ceremonies involved more than a loaf of bread and jug of wine, if you get my drift—witness the unfortunately well-worn altar stone.

"Shortest way to the kennels without cutting through the ceilidh glade or getting too close to the Keep," Frang rumbled.

I tried not to trip over my own feet as I trailed along at the rear of our merry band, although it was tough considering I couldn't stop goggling at the ring of giant menhirs and that sinister altar stone. My fingers itched to take out my camera and capture a few shots against the violet sky, bright stars, and too-close-to-be-real Faerie moon.

But I knew better. Because those photos could be used as evidence that I'd violated the letter of my…parole, I guess you'd call it. No human had ever set foot inside the Circle unless they weren't coming out again, if you follow me, and although this was the new and improved Faerie, fae were notoriously resistant to change. I didn't want to be a test case for the upgrade to that particular situation, especially while under probation.

"*Ooof*," I grunted, having run into Eleri's back and extremely pointed elbow. "Warn a guy, can't you?" I tore my gaze away from the altar and my mouth dropped open.

There in front of us stood enormous double wooden doors. And when I say enormous, I'm talking huge. At least three times Frang's height, and if you haven't gotten the picture yet, he's not exactly a candidate for the Lollipop Guild.

But it wasn't the size of the doors that was the most startling. No, that would be because they weren't attached to a visible building or fence. They were just standing there, on their own, in the sparse woods beyond the plateau.

"Wow," Jordan breathed. "Those things are really big."

Master of understatement, our Jordan.

Frang jerked his thumb at them. "Kennels're beyond the gates."

"Okay." I had my doubts about my ability to open anything that massive, but Frang's muscles had muscles. "Do we knock, or can you just open the door?"

He crossed his arms, which should have looked threatening, but given the way the whites of his eyes were showing again, I suspected he was trying to hold himself together, literally. "I brought you here, but I'm not going in."

"Why not?"

He edged further away from Doop, who was attempting to sniff Jordan's butt again. "One hellhound is bad enough. A whole pack of them?" He shook his head. "Not chancing it."

"Don't call him a hellhound," Jordan said while pushing Doop's muzzle away from his butt. "You'll hurt his feelings."

I tried to muster some authority. "Frang, you know I need your escort for this."

He shook his head mulishly. "I took you this far. No farther."

"Will you at least wait to take us back? On the clock, of course."

"It's your gold," he said. "I'll wait back at the Circle." He backed away, never taking his eyes off Doop. "But if you're not out in half an hour, I'm gone. My fare doesn't cover cleaning up *that* kind of mess." With one final glance at Doop, he turned to lumber back down the path and disappear into the trees.

"Well, *that* was weird," Eleri said tartly. "Whoever heard of a nervous duergar?"

"Guess you don't know everything after all," I said with a grin.

She sniffed. "Still know more than you."

"No argument there." I glanced from the gates to Doop and frowned. "This close to his kennel—and presumably his dinner —you'd think he'd be less interested in Jordan's behind than in storming the gates."

She shrugged. "He's probably used to waiting until they're opened. It's not as though he's got the ability to push..." She narrowed her eyes at the gates. "Wait a minute." She crept forward like a stalking cat. When she reached the gates, she reached out and pushed the left one with a finger.

It moved.

"These are unlocked and open," she said, her voice low. "That *never* happens unless the Hunt is riding."

I glanced around wildly, half expecting the whole pack of *Cwn Annwn*, accompanied by Herne the Horned Hunter, to burst out of the trees and take us all into custody. Or worse.

But the woods were silent. Not a rustle, not a cheep, not a crack, as if I were wearing my noise-canceling headphones. "Does the pack ever hunt without Herne?"

"Sometimes." She peered through the gap in the doors. "They can be called out for security within Faerie, but I haven't heard of that happening since before the Convergence."

The Convergence. The ceremony where the Seelie and Unseelie spheres were remade into one big maybe-not-so-happy Faerie, if Frang's gossip was on point.

"Do you suppose that's how Doop got out?" I asked.

"Could be. Although why the kennel master didn't notice and raise the alarm?" She shrugged.

"Well." I gripped my camera bag strap since I didn't have anything else to hold on to. "Let's go return his AWOL hound to him and ask him what's up."

Eleri slipped through the gap. I turned to invite Jordan to lead Doop inside, but Doop's eyes were wilder than Frang's had been. He dropped to his haunches, whining.

Jordan crouched next to him. "He doesn't want to go in there."

"You think?" I sighed. "Fine. I'm sure the kennel master will know how to entice him. Will you stay out here with him to make sure he doesn't run off again?"

He nodded. "Sure." He brightened and grabbed a stick the length of his forearm off the ground. "It's not as good as a Frisbee, but maybe I can teach him to play fetch with this."

I lifted an eyebrow. "He probably knows how to fetch already. Although I doubt it's anything as innocuous or inanimate as a stick."

"Oh." Jordan glanced sidelong at Doop, who had crept further away from the gates. "I guess that's why Frang's so freaked out, huh?"

"I expect so."

Eleri poked her head out of the gates. "Are you guys coming? The meter's running on Frang's patience."

"Right." I patted Jordan's shoulder. "Thanks. We'll try not to take too long."

"It's okay. I don't mind waiting." He sat down and crossed his legs tailor-fashion. "Especially not when I've got company." He patted his knee and Doop crept toward him, belly brushing the ground, to lay his head in Jordan's lap and heave a huge doggy sigh. "Maybe ask the kennel master why he's so cold?" He ran his fingers along Doop's spine, causing the dog's leg to paddle. "I'm worried that he might be sick."

"You bet." I hurried over to the gates and slipped through to join Eleri on the other side.

And inside was an entirely different scene than outside. I'm not sure why that surprised me. I mean, I told you about Faerie's changing geography and the pocket dimensions which, although they're now licensed by Sheol to use in the Upper World, weren't exclusive to Sheol originally. There are supe firms who handle alternate dimension architecture, for Pete's sake. They're the ones who maintain the supe-only wings of United Memorial Hospital—which supes refer to as St. Stupid's for some reason. I mean, there's an entire six-story-plus-multiple-basement-levels hospital *right there*, but humans have no clue it exists.

Magic. Go figure.

Anyway, the kennel gates weren't free-standing in the middle of the woods anymore. Inside, they were part of a palisade that enclosed a compound at least the size of a couple of side-by-side football fields. Several structures were located about a third of the way across—one was a small cottage, although no smoke curled from its chimney. The others, judging by their sprawling footprints and adjacent fenced enclosures, were clearly the kennels and probably a stable. Herne rode a horse, right? The horse had to live somewhere unless Herne kept his mount with him wherever he hung out in between hunts.

One building was taller, with a definite barn vibe and an obvious second story. A hayloft maybe? The other was longer and lower and no doubt housed the hounds. The buildings were constructed of rough gray stone and roofed with thatch, but other than the materials, they could have been lifted from any farm or dog breeder in the Outer World.

I should probably mention these directional references, huh? The way that the various supernatural races refer to the human realm depends entirely on their own context. With Sheol, since it's, you know, down *there*, the human realm is the Upper World. Since Faerie is an artificial construct inside its own magical bubble, it's the Outer World. For werewolves, who live within the human realm but—at least in the past—somewhat isolated from it within their own pack compounds, it's the Wider World. For all I know, the former Angelic Host (now just part of the unified Host) who reside in Elysium refer to it as the Lower World, although I've never spoken to one of them long enough to ask the question. The only angel I'd ever met—and that only briefly—was such a jerk I wouldn't ask him the way to the nearest Starbucks.

Not that he would have answered if I had. Angels have a real holier-than-thou problem.

I peered around in the moonlight. With the moon past full, it wasn't as bright as it would have been under a full moon, but here in Faerie, it was bigger and more luminous than it appeared in the Outer World. Mal's brother-in-law, my friend David, told me once that even though Faerie shared the same sun, moon, and stars as the Outer World, in Faerie, size and brightness were based on relative importance, not physical characteristics.

Hence the moon, though gibbous, lighted the place better than my Target lamps lit my bedroom. So I couldn't blame darkness on the fact that I could detect zero movement anywhere. And the silence in here was even more profound than it had been outside the gates.

And if I told you that didn't freak me out? I'd be lying.

"Something's wrong," I murmured to Eleri, reluctant to break the eerie silence.

"No shit, Sherlock," she whispered back fiercely.

"Have you been here before?"

She nodded and swallowed audibly. "Once. I came in with a work crew from my clan. The dryads take it in turns to maintain the roof thatch."

"Was it this quiet then?"

"No. It was just as chaotic as you'd expect a kennel and a stable to be. Dogs barking. Trainers taking the horses and hounds through their paces. Lesser fae scuttling around with water buckets and food pails. It was *busy*." She swallowed again as though she were suppressing either sobs or nervous giggles. "It was *cheerful*, which you'd never expect from the home of a pack of dogs that, Jordan's opinion notwithstanding, most non-Welsh folk refer to as hellhounds."

"Doesn't look so cheerful now. Or busy." In fact, it looked abandoned. "Could Herne or the kennel master have decided to relocate? I mean, so many other things are changing. Now that there's real estate available in the former Unseelie sphere, maybe there's a better spot?"

Her exasperated glance was tempered with obvious fear. "This is Faerie. If the spot isn't good, just ask and it'll get better.

Besides, Sawyl, the kennel master, always said this place was well-suited."

"You know Sawyl?"

"A little. They're a bauchan and they mostly keep to this compound, though, so I haven't seen them often. I don't winter in Faerie like a lot of my clan do." She snorted. "Another reason my clan chief looks at me like I'm a three-headed demon who rides a crocodile. But the dormant season in the Pacific Northwest isn't as severe as it is in other places, so why would I uproot myself for half the year?"

"I couldn't say." It was my turn to swallow noisily. "Should we check out the buildings? See if we can find a clue about where everybody went?"

"Might as well." She glanced over her shoulder and shivered. "Although if this is what Doop was running from, no wonder he preferred the Burgervilles."

I took out my camera. I know, I know. I said I didn't want to risk an accidental probation violation. But with phantom spiders creeping along my spine, I had this *feeling*, you know? That documenting everything before we contaminated it by merely searching through it would be important.

I mounted the special bespelled lens that let me photograph in low-light situations, but cursed inwardly at the loss of my telephoto. To get any more detailed close-up shots, we'd need to be, well, close up. "Wait a sec while I take a few wide shots." She nodded, familiar enough now with my methods not to question me. She stayed silent in the eerie quiet as I worked. "Which building should we start with? The kennel or the cottage?"

Her brow puckered in thought. "Kennel. That's why we came, so nobody would question us entering without an express invitation. If we don't find anything there, we can try the cottage." She worried her lower lip with her teeth. "Although there are no lights inside."

There were no lights anywhere, for that matter. Only the moon and stars.

We crossed the deserted grounds. Since Eleri could move through any vegetation absolutely silently, my footsteps swishing in the grass were the only sounds. Like the gates, the kennel double doors were almost closed but not latched. I kept a supply of nitrile gloves in my camera bag, because you never knew. I passed a pair to Eleri and worked my hands into my own.

"You really think this is necessary?" she asked, screwing her face up at the crumpled gloves.

"I'm a human on probation, in a place where I was explicitly told not to go. Better safe than sorry."

"Good point."

I pushed one door and she pushed the other. They opened without a single creak or groan, and seriously? All this soundlessness was really getting to me. I was tempted to shout just to see if I could raise an echo. On the other hand, if there really *was* something sinister going on, I didn't want to attract anyone's attention.

"We're going to feel really stupid if we creep in here and find out they've all gone to Aruba on vacay," I muttered.

Eleri rolled her eyes. "Yeah, because nobody would notice a couple dozen giant white hounds, a short person with greenish pebbly skin and green hair, and a tall dude with horns sprouting out of his head, sipping pina coladas on the beach."

We walked past empty pen after empty pen. Well, empty of dogs. Each of them held bedding and a water bowl—all dry—but nothing else. "Where do they feed the dogs?"

"Out back. I've heard it's part of their training, so they're never just *given* the food."

I frowned. "That doesn't seem very humane."

"That's because nobody here is human, doofus." She sighed. "But you're right. The *Cwn Annwn* live almost as austerely as

Herne. Keeps them from bonding with somebody they might have to kill someday."

My stomach roiled. *Ugh.* "Thanks for that."

"Hey. Nobody ever said the fae were sweet and fluffy. *Implacable* is more our speed."

I remembered the extended dryad hazing that had resulted from the case where I'd first encountered Eleri. "You can say that again."

At the end of the row of pens, the kennels opened up into a square room, two of its walls lined with neat shelves and lidded bins. A third sported pegs that held a smorgasbord of tools, presumably related to dog and pony care. If I remembered the outside layout correctly, the enormous sliding doors in the fourth wall opened onto the fenced dog run.

The room held one other thing that probably hadn't been part of the original building spec.

The crumpled body of a bauchan, their green hair streaked with white, their dark eyes filming over, but obviously widened in fear or pain.

From the scorched hole in the front of their canvas coverall? I didn't think they'd expired from natural causes.

CHAPTER NINE

The five of us—me, Eleri, Jordan, Frang, and Doop—huddled under an elm tree outside the kennel gates with a trio of the King's guards looming over us. After we'd raised the alarm by contacting Zeke with Jordan's not-exactly-sanctioned text app, the cavalry had arrived in force: Niall, Mal, the *King*, for crying out loud, along with a whole phalanx of other fae.

"They're completely compromising the crime scene," I muttered, fiddling with the zipper on my camera bag where it sat next to me on the lush grass.

"How do you know it was a crime scene?" Eleri asked. She was sitting closer to me than usual. I think the guards were freaking her out a little, although not as much as Doop continued to freak out Frang.

"Hello? Hole scorched in his coverall? Can the *Cwn Annwn* shoot lasers from their glowing eyes too?"

"Of course not," she huffed. "But we didn't get a look at his chest *under* his coveralls, so maybe it was pre-existing damage."

"From what? A fire-breathing stable rat?"

"No, the damage would be lower then. Ankle height."

I goggled at her. "You're kidding. There really *are* fire-breathing stable rats?"

"What do you think?" She shivered and edged closer. "I'm sorry. Snark is my defense mechanism. But if he was killed here, in Faerie, in the kennel palisade, which is even more secure than the Keep, what does that mean for the rest of us? There hasn't been a murder in Faerie since the Tor Massacre two hundred years ago."

I frowned at her. "Really? I thought the old Unseelie King made a habit of ridding himself of anybody who disagreed with him."

"Oh, there have been royally decreed executions, but those at least had an understandable context, even if they were complete bullshit. This, though?" She shivered. "Nothing as random and up close and personal as this."

"So you agree it's a crime scene?"

She nodded. "But I don't want it to be."

I sighed and gave her a one-armed hug. That was one of the problems of being in the investigation business. If you were working, it meant somebody had stepped out of line, and wishing everybody could just get along with each other didn't make a damn bit of difference. Frankly, it could get a little depressing, especially to someone like me who was still star-struck over the mere existence of the supernatural.

I was thrilled it was real, but I wanted it to be *good* too. And it wasn't. Not always.

Mal emerged from the gates, his hand on the shoulder of a sobbing bauchan. He didn't even look our way—just disappeared down the path with the person, murmuring softly in an extremely un-Mal-like fashion.

"Do you know who that is?" I asked Eleri.

"Heilyn. They work in the Keep. They've got a close friendship with Mal and Bryce, a sort of mutual admiration society. I think"—she swallowed what sounded suspiciously like a sob—"they're related to Sawyl."

"Really? How? Parent? Sibling?"

She shrugged listlessly. "Other than parent/child, it's hard to assign relationship labels to bauchan. Their reproduction is... interesting, each of them producing one multiple birth from pods on their back that are present when they're born themselves. Nobody really knows what triggers the babies to mature enough to emerge. The bauchan aren't telling." She sighed. "They might not even know themselves."

I gazed at the spot where Mal and Heilyn had disappeared. This was fascinating stuff, and ordinarily I'd be taking notes like mad. But my curiosity about all things supe was orders of magnitude less important than Heilyn's sorrow.

The most significant thing I could do for them was to help find their relative's killer—or killers—and bring them to justice.

An honor guard of high fae emerged from the gates, their pace measured, their expressions somber. They bore a litter with Sawyl's pitiful body draped in a swath of green silk embroidered with gold. The King followed the bier, even more somber than the pallbearers. None of them glanced our way, either.

I frowned as they disappeared in the same direction as Mal. "Why would anyone target Sawyl?" I murmured.

"Yeah, and where are the other dogs?" Jordan sounded more subdued than I'd ever heard him.

"Good questions, both."

All of us started at Niall's comment. You'd think a six-foot-plus guy with a chest like a WWE star and sporting boots that could pass muster in a *Bridgertons* episode wouldn't be able to sneak up on all of us—Doop included. He'd arrived as silently as if he'd teleported, and so far, I hadn't heard of any supe with *that* particular ability.

Although...

I listened hard and couldn't hear anything outside our little circle now that Heilyn's sobs had faded. Were we encased in some kind of Cone of Silence spell? I'd encountered weirder things in the last year, trust me.

Niall looked even grimmer than his brother had. "Hugh, could you come with me, please?"

Uh oh. Here it came—my Quest pink slip and appointment with the supe council for selective memory adjustment. But I'd walked into this one with my eyes open, so although it knifed me in the gut to know I'd soon lose all of this—my job, my friends, my knowledge of this world—I couldn't argue with the consequences.

I nodded and pushed myself to my feet. But then he surprised me, because he said, "Bring your camera."

I grabbed the bag and hurried after him as he strode for the gates. Did he need to wipe the camera's memory as well as my own? But when we got inside—that hidden vista opening up again—he stopped, shoulders slumping, and carded his fingers through his hair.

"Shite," he muttered.

"Niall?" I asked tentatively. "Are you angry?"

He lifted his head, eyes blazing. "Angry? That's a bloody understatement. I'm furious. Enraged. Bloody *livid*."

"I'm sorry. I know I was supposed to stick to the paths, but we had to return the dog, and—"

"I'm not angry with *you*, Hugh. *Matt*." He gripped my shoulder. "Your actions are completely defensible under the terms of your probation. You made your decisions to preserve the Secrecy Pact and your FTA driver accompanied you. I might have wished for a little advance notice." A shadow of a smile flitted across his face. "But my anger is aimed entirely at whoever had the unmitigated gall, the pure *evil* to murder an inoffensive bauchan, a loyal fae who'd never done anything other than excel at their job."

"So it was murder then?"

He nodded. "Yes. Zeke said you'd taken pictures of where Sawyl's body was found."

"Yes. Although I didn't have a chance to take many of the body itself. Zeke warned me to stand down until you and the King could arrive."

He narrowed his eyes. "I wish he hadn't done that." Obviously twigging that I was about to protest and defend Zeke, he raised his hands, palms out. "I understand why he did, and it's certainly standard protocol for incidents inside Faerie." This time, his smile landed, albeit crooked and wry. "Quest's purview is the Outer World. The King and Queen hold all investigative jurisdiction here. But I suspect they'll be handing this case to us, anyway."

"Because we're good at what we do?"

"Not entirely. This way." He led me to a spot to the left of the gates and pointed to a scorch mark in the grass. "I suspect that where you discovered Sawyl was not, in fact, where they were killed. This has the same etheric signature as the burn on their coverall."

"So whoever did it moved them? But why?"

"When we find the bastards," he said, his voice steely, "we'll ask them. And trust me when I tell you that they *will* answer."

I was seeing Niall and Mal—my iconoclastic bosses, the snarky, irreverent mavericks of Faerie—in a very different light tonight. I'd never seen Mal as a comforter nor Niall as an avenger. But apparently they had more facets than I'd ever known.

"Do you, um, have a suspect?"

His eyes narrowed to slits. "Only two people can open those gates. Two, and one of them is dead. Not even the King or Queen can enter unescorted because the *Cwn Annwn* are ancillary, like Herne himself. Meta-Faerie, if you will. Not subject to the monarchs' rule, since they might, when pursuing their rightful prey, be called on to bring down the monarchs themselves." His lips pressed together in a thin line. "As they did when hunting my father."

Right. Niall had personal experience with the Wild Hunt. I gulped. "You suspect Herne, then?"

"Who else could enter with impunity and leave again with *the entire pack* of *Cwn Annwn*? I can see Sawyl perhaps opening the gates for someone else if they believed the visitor had legitimate business. But no hound would go anywhere outside the compound with anyone other than Herne."

I jerked my chin at the open gates, where Jordan sat next to Eleri with Doop doing his best to sit in his lap. "One hound went somewhere else."

Niall's eyebrows rose. "A point. I wonder if that was simply an oversight on Herne's part because this dog is too young to course with the pack? Ordinarily, the pups and younger animals are kept in a separate run until they're fully trained."

"So you think Doop was just...forgotten?"

Niall's eyebrows shot up further. "*What* did you call him?"

I grimaced. "Sorry. Eleri referred to him as *ci dwp*. Jordan misunderstood the Welsh and started calling him Doop. It stuck."

Niall chuckled softly. "Yet somehow he managed to flit in and out of Faerie to search for food in the Outer World. It strikes me that he's the polar opposite of *dwp*."

I chuckled too, even though my chest was tight. If the gates hadn't been left ajar, if Doop hadn't found his way to those Burgervilles, to *us*, he might have been trapped in here alone and starved to death. It didn't bear thinking of, so I pushed it aside. "You want me to document the scene?"

He nodded. "As much as you can, given that our big fae feet have trampled all over the evidence by now."

"Got it. I'll—" I caught sight of Frang pushing heavily to his feet. "Holy crap. Frang! The meter's still running on our trip." How long had it been? I'd lost track and checking my watch wouldn't help, considering Faerie's *flexible* relationship with time. "I'm sorry, Niall. This is gonna run into some serious gold."

He patted my shoulder. "Don't worry. I'll square things with Frang." He took a deep breath, wide chest lifting. "I'll need to speak with my brother, too, so when you're finished here, please return to the office. I'll meet you there to debrief."

"All of us?"

He studied the little group outside the gate. "Other than Frang? All of you." He shook his head. "Goddess help us all."

CHAPTER
TEN

"Doop! Put that down!" Jordan hurried across the room to where Doop was growling and shaking his head, something clamped between his teeth.

We'd only gotten back to the offices a few minutes ago and had shut the dog in the Little Conference Room—much to Doop's disapproval, if the scratches and whines were any indication. But all of us had needed a bathroom break.

Apparently, the five minutes it had taken us to do our business was all the time it had taken for Doop to cause a little mayhem.

Eleri collapsed on the loveseat in the corner while Jordan tried to convince Doop to turn over whatever he was savaging. "What's he got, anyway?"

"That jerkin I wore out of Faerie," Jordan said absently. "Drop it, Doop!" Surprisingly, Doop dropped it, then flung himself on his side like a canine drama queen. Jordan picked it up with two fingers, holding it his entire arm's-length away. "I took it home and washed it." He wrinkled his nose as he refolded it. "I guess I shouldn't have put it in the dryer. It's not really the same." He gave Doop as severe a look as I'd ever seen on his face. "But that doesn't mean it should be a chew toy."

Doop just sighed heavily and rolled onto his belly, dropping his head on his paws in a doggy mope.

Jordan crouched next to him, petting his silky red ears—and when I say *red*, I don't mean Irish Setter rufous. Nope. Doop's ears were the red of fresh blood. "I think he wants more sweet potato fries."

I glanced up from unloading my camera bag onto the table. "Whether he wants them or not, I doubt they're good for him, even assuming you could acquire any. It's almost three in the morning and no Burgerville has 24-hour drive-through service."

Jordan sighed gustily. "I guess. But he's got to be hungry. We need to feed him *something*." He scratched Doop's back. "What do you suppose hellhounds eat normally?"

"I thought we weren't allowed to call him a hellhound for fear of hurting his feelings," I said absently.

"I don't think he minds. Do you, boy?" Jordan crooned. "So what does the pack eat?"

Eleri canted an eyebrow. "The flesh of traitors."

Jordan's mouth dropped open and he shuddered. "That's just...*ewww*."

Eleri shrugged. "It's what the *Cwn Annwn* were bred for. You can't blame them."

"I'm not *blaming* them, but *jeez*."

Jordan had picked that term up from me. "The kid's got a point. I doubt any of the dog food brands in your average PetSmart feature the flesh of traitors as their first ingredient." Or any ingredient, for that matter.

Eleri smirked. "Bet you could find something online."

I held up my hands, palms out. "Not even tempted to load that into my browser search window, thanks. I'm already on thin ice with the council. I don't need the human authorities on my case, too. Besides, if he was stalking that delivery truck and haunting Burgerville dumpsters, Doop is clearly on board with an alternative diet."

Doop's head popped up, his nose quivering, and an instant later Zeke walked in with a tray, although it didn't hold the tea or coffee service this time: It held a big bowl of what looked like meat scraps. Doop scrambled to his feet and headed toward Zeke, tail wagging as he circled behind the demon.

"Doop!" Jordan said sharply. "No butt sniffing!"

Doop's tail wilted, but he stopped aiming his muzzle at Zeke's backside. Instead, he sat, ears pricked attentively.

"Aw," Eleri said, fluttering her eyelashes at Jordan, "look at that, Hugh. Our little boy is growing up and going all alpha."

"I'm not an alpha," Jordan said, a blush staining his cheeks. "I'm not even alpha *potential.*"

Zeke smiled at him fondly. "You're the one Doop listens to, though, so to him, you're the alpha." He set the tray on the table and picked up the bowl, but instead of setting it on the floor for the dog, he handed it to Jordan. "So let's reinforce that notion, shall we?"

Jordan gazed at him, wide-eyed, as he accepted the bowl. "Really?" At Zeke's nod, Jordan straightened his shoulders, chin high, and set the bowl on the floor, a good six feet from Doop, who was almost vibrating even though he stayed where he'd sat at Jordan's last command.

"Stay... stay... stay," Jordan drawled, teasing out the words. Then he gestured sharply to the bowl with two fingers. "Take it!"

Doop lunged for the meat and started—heh—wolfing it down.

"I'll refill his water bowl," Zeke said, but Jordan stopped him with a hand on his arm.

"That's okay, Zeke. I'll take care of it." Jordan was practically glowing with pride. "He's my responsibility."

As he trotted out of the room with the water bowl, I shared an astonished glance with Eleri. "What is happening right now?"

She laughed. "Like I said, our little wolfboy is growing up." She shrugged. "Had to happen sometime."

"If you say so."

Jordan returned with the bowl, water sloshing over the sides to dribble a trail across the floor. I shook my head, chuckling. He was making progress, but he still had a way to go to qualify as *all grown up*.

He sat down cross-legged next to Doop, who'd scarfed down the meat and was now drinking noisily. Jordan met my gaze seriously. "He can't stay here."

"Really?" Eleri said. "I figured Zeke was getting bored with answering a gazillion wrong numbers every day and needed something to do with all his spare time. Taking care of a hellhound should be a piece of cake for a demon."

"I was never trained in animal care," Zeke said diffidently. "But I suppose I could—"

"Hey!" Eleri leaped up and ran over to give Zeke a hug. "I was only joking. You do way too much for us already." She kissed his cheek and Zeke's blotchy blush polka-dotted his pale skin.

"I'm just doing my job," he said.

"I'm pretty sure being on duty all day *and* all night is beyond the call of any job," I said, smiling at him as I popped the memory card out of my camera. "You don't have to stay here for us. We can manage. We're just waiting on Niall before we head out ourselves." I stifled a yawn. "I hope he won't get tied up with his brother for long."

Suddenly, Jordan stood up. "I'm taking Doop home," he announced.

Eleri raised her eyebrows. "Home where? There's nobody at the kennels."

"Not *there*. It's creepy and he needs a *pack*. I'm taking him to *my* home. The Howling Residence. The other guys won't mind."

"Well, it is called the Dog House," I drawled, and Eleri snorted.

"Come *on*," Jordan snapped, and the uncharacteristic edge in his tone made Eleri and me both straighten. "I know Niall doesn't really want to talk to *me*. I'll just sit here while you two report. At least if I'm taking care of Doop, I'll be doing something useful."

"Jordan," I said, "if we've made you feel like you're in our way, or that we don't value you—"

"It's okay," he said with a tight smile. "I know I've got a lot to learn. But I want to *try*, you know? Get better. Find my place."

This time, Eleri hugged Jordan. "You will, sweetie. You totally will."

"I think taking Doop to the Dog House is an excellent idea," Zeke said. "I'm sure Niall *will* want to chat with you, but that can certainly wait until tomorrow." He glanced at the camelback clock on the credenza. "Well, later today, at any rate."

I'd been to the Dog House, though, so I had questions. "You've got something in the kitchen besides pizza, right?"

Jordan gave me a look that rivaled Zeke's former angel nemesis for disdain. "I'm a *werewolf*, Hugh. I know what kind of nutrition canines need." Then he grinned. "Even if we ignore it sometimes in favor of the good human stuff." He patted his thigh. "Come, Doop."

Doop lurched to his giant paws, his tail wagging in an arc so enthusiastic it swept the folded clothing onto the floor and nearly sent my camera bag after it. I leaped up to rescue the bag before Doop's tail could make the return trip.

Jordan lifted his hand in farewell, his usual open grin tempered by something that might actually be *responsibility*. "See you guys later."

He trotted out with Doop prancing at his heels, gazing up at him in adoration. I set my bag back on the table. "How exactly is he getting back to the Dog House with an animal that size?"

Zeke blinked. "Oh. They ought to have a—"

"Hey, Zeke?" Jordan poked his head through the door. "Do you have anything I could use for a collar and leash? I don't want Doop to get excited and run out into traffic."

Eleri grinned. "He's way ahead of you, Zeke."

"Or at least running neck and neck," I said as Zeke hustled off with Jordan and Doop. "Zeke's good, but do you suppose he's really got a leash equivalent stocked up that'll fit Doop? Or any leash equivalent at all?"

She shrugged and wandered over to inspect the plate of scones on the credenza. "We're talking about Zeke. He's probably got something stashed in one of those dimensional storage pockets of his that'll work just fine." She picked up a poppyseed scone. "Wonder how Doop missed these?"

I stooped and picked up the borrowed trousers. "I've gotta admit, for a hellhound last seen scrounging food behind a Burgerville—"

"Burger*villes*," she said around a mouthful of scone. "Doop was an equal opportunity scrounger."

"Fine. Burger*villes*. As I was saying, he's really remarkably well-behaved, if a little over-enthusiastic."

She grinned. "In other words, he's Jordan."

"That's…an excellent point." I shook out the trousers and held them up, studying them critically. "I suggest we never enlist Doop to do the laundry then. Jordan must have washed these things in hot water." The leather trousers, which were originally a fawn color, now had a decidedly pinkish tinge. "With a pair of red socks." I folded the pants and set them on the table just as Niall strode in, looking grim.

"Everything okay?" I asked, and then winced. Of course everything wasn't okay. Sawyl was dead. "Have you located the rest of the pack?"

He shook his head. "No. And none of the diviners can scry their whereabouts either."

"That's not unusual, though, is it?" Eleri asked, abandoning the scones to perch on the edge of the table. "If they're with Herne, they'd be cloaked."

"Cloaked?" I asked.

"When Herne is hunting," Niall said, "he is himself untrackable." He lifted a sardonic eyebrow. "It somewhat reduces the efficacy, not to mention the terror, of being his prey if you can see him coming."

"So I'm guessing you can't find Herne either?" I picked up the jerkin. After Jordan's laundry adventures and Doop's determination to chew it into submission, it was pretty much DOA. Then again, since Grizel only handled the washing of the soon-to-be-deceased, I doubted if its owner would need it again. "Have you checked his...house? Lair? Whatever?"

"Nobody just drops in on Herne. You don't go to him. He comes to you."

"I'm guessing he doesn't get a lot of party invites then," I said as I tried to smooth Doop-induced creases from the jerkin, "considering how poorly party behavior can reflect on—"

Niall snatched the jerkin out of my hands and stared at it intently. "Where did you get this?"

"It was hanging on Grizel's tree. I ran face-first into it when Jordan knocked me off balance. We borrowed it so he wouldn't be naked on the way back to the office after she forced him to shift back." Now that I thought of it, maybe dressing Jordan in what amounted to a dead man's clothes was kind of creepy. What if... My belly dropped. If Jordan had worn the clothes, did that mean he would share the same fate? They weren't technically *his* clothes. They certainly hadn't been when Grizel had been hanging them up on the tree.

Niall's jaw sagged, his fist tightening on the jerkin. "Wait. You saw *Grizel*? Talked to her? *Touched* her washing?"

I shared a bewildered glance with Eleri. "Well, yeah. You know we did. She lodged that complaint against us."

Niall pinched the bridge of his nose, something he did whenever he was trying not to let his temper get the better of him. I'd noticed he did that a lot whenever Jordan was around. "Grizel didn't lodge the complaints."

The glance Eleri and I exchanged this time was more guilty than bewildered. "Complaints?" she asked. "There was more than one?"

"Two," Niall replied. "One from a dryad who claimed that trees had been disarranged."

"Honestly," Eleri said, flopping back in the loveseat and crossing her arms. "The OG dryads are just so…so *petrified*."

I lifted my eyebrows. None of the dryads I'd ever met had struck me as timorous. "What are they afraid of?"

"Not *that* kind of petrified. The *other* kind." She held her arms out, elbows bent like goalposts. "They might as well be made of stone. Or…or *plastic*. I mean, hello? New growth? They really need to embrace it."

Eleri seemed like she was about to sprout a little new growth of her own, and when she got in a snit, that usually involved thorns. Really big ones. Zeke had enough to do without having to repair the upholstery, too, so I threw myself into the breach.

"I take it the other complaint was about me?"

Niall nodded. "I'm afraid so. A courtier from the former Seelie sphere. After the Convergence, his valet left to take a job at St. Stupid's for better pay—well, for pay period, since his stroppy lordship didn't actually provide anything but room and board."

"Why is that my problem?"

Niall's smile was wry. "It's not. Or only in that you're a symbol of change. A very obvious symbol." He lifted an eyebrow. "An often indiscreet symbol. But let's return to the main question." He draped the jerkin over a chair back. "You took this from Grizel?" His attention zeroed in on me, and when Niall *looks* at you with that intensity? Well, it makes an impression. Lying wasn't an option, even if I'd been inclined, which I wasn't.

I mean, I avoided questions sometimes, or simply omitted certain things—like the reason I'd been stalking Grizel in the first place, for instance. I doubted Niall would be impressed by that particular strategy for scoring a date.

On the other hand, his entire two-centuries-long-and-counting love affair with Gareth Kendrick—Mal's brother and the last true bard of Faerie—had been based on deception, if not outright lies. Who better to understand my motives? So I copped to the whole thing.

"You know Wyn still hasn't surfaced since he vanished last month."

"I'm aware," he drawled.

"Lachlan can't move on until they've had their sundering ceremony. He won't cheat, not as long as he's technically still handfasted even if they've both decided the marriage is over." I swallowed thickly, wishing for some of Zeke's stellar coffee. Or maybe a cup of hemlock. Eleri could probably manage that. She'd just need to chat with one of her tree friends. "Since I was with Mal when he questioned Grizel about Tanner Araya's whereabouts last spring, I thought she would be the most reliable source of information about where to find Wyn."

"You thought..." Niall's voice was strained. "Grizel? *Reliable?* Danu's tits, man, she's a *bean-nighe.*"

"I know that," I said tartly. "I'd worked out my questions so they couldn't be misinterpreted, and—"

Niall laughed. And laughed. And laughed, the big royal jerk. "Sorry," he said, wiping a tear away. "Every *bean-nighe* prides herself on *never* giving a straight answer. No matter how you'd phrased it, Grizel would have found a way to twist the response." He choked out another laugh. "The only defense is being as squirrelly as she is, which is why Mal and I can get on with her after a fashion. But you two?" He glanced down at the jerkin. "Three, considering Jordan was there, too. You're no better than toddlers playing on the train tracks."

"Hey!" Eleri and I said in unison.

Niall shook his head. "No disrespect to you. But Grizel is on an entirely different level." He pointed to the jerkin. "And she was definitely hanging this out to dry?"

I nodded. "I got tangled in it when Jordan knocked me sideways. Why?"

He gazed down at the jerkin, tracing the pattern embroidered on its breast. "Because I recognize this." He raised his chin and met our eyes. "It belongs to Herne."

CHAPTER ELEVEN

For a full minute, neither Eleri nor I could do anything but goggle at him. Finally, I managed to croak, "It's *Herne's*? As in Herne the Hunter, scourge of traitors, leader of the pack?" Niall nodded. "How can you tell?"

He tapped the gold embroidery on the left of the collar lacing. "This is his badge."

"Wait. Herne wears a *name badge*? Like Bob the delivery driver?"

"Think of it more as a badge of authority. Proving he has the right—"

"To kick your ass," Eleri said.

I stared at the jerkin. "So if Grizel's hanging up Herne's drawers, does that mean he's..." I swallowed again. Dammit, where was Zeke? He had a sixth sense about when we needed coffee. I was surprised he hadn't shown up five minutes ago. "Is Herne already dead?"

Niall smoothed the jerkin's creases almost gently. "I don't think so. She's a harbinger. She doesn't kill people directly. But if she's already hanging Herne out to dry, as it were, I'm pretty sure the die has been cast."

"Unfortunate choice of words, Niall," I muttered as I edged closer to the table and gazed at the shrunken garments. "If she's got his clothes, and he's not dead, what? Is he just lounging around in his skivvies?"

"I'm pretty sure those were hanging on the tree too," Eleri said. "But taking those seemed a little too squicky. Jordan went commando."

"These aren't—or at least they weren't—his literal clothes. They're more…metaphorical. Or at least they were before Jordan washed them with a lack of notable skill."

"Does she have to complete the job?" I asked. "I mean, if we've got these…these ex-metaphorical duds, does that mean Herne's fate isn't sealed? Can she…" What was the verb form of *harbinger*? "…harbinge without them?"

Niall frowned, his perfect eyebrows drawing together. "I don't believe it's ever happened before. I don't know what it means and I don't know what will happen. But I know one thing." His jaw tightened. "We need to find Herne immediately. Because right now, he's the prime suspect in Sawyl's murder. And if he did that—if he slaughtered the person who's been his most loyal retainer for eons—he's committed the biggest betrayal of all. He could be his own prey, which might be why he's absconded with the *Cwn Annwn* and gone into hiding."

"You think that might be why Grizel's predicting his demise via clothesline?" I asked as Zeke bustled in with the coffee service, thank goodness. "Because he's about to be executed for his crimes? How soon does death follow Grizel's laundry day?"

Niall shrugged. "Nobody's ever collected that particular data." He gave Eleri and me a severe glare. "Because *mostly* nobody's foolhardy enough to seek her out."

"Yeah, yeah. We've got that memo." I accepted a cup of coffee from Zeke. "Thanks, man. You're an angel."

He smiled, his blush splotching his cheeks. "No, just one of the Host."

Eleri doctored her coffee with more raw sugar than should be allowed. "But you said nobody can just drop in on Herne, even when he's not allegedly in hiding. How can we speak to him?"

A muscle ticked in Niall's jaw. "There's only one way. The one summons he can't ignore or refuse."

Zeke dropped a teaspoon onto the silver tray with a clatter. His eyes were wide behind his glasses. "The horn?" he whispered.

Niall nodded. "Blow on Herne's horn and he'll answer."

"Okay." I glanced between the other three, all of whom were looking a little green. "So we blow the horn. What's the big deal?"

"The deal," Eleri said, her voice tight, "is that blowing that horn launches the Wild Hunt. Herne shows up, yeah, but then you have to point him at his rightful prey, and if you don't?" She plucked at the leaf-patterned leggings under her denim skirt with fingers gone twiggy. "He finds one of his own."

"And he's not one to quibble over gray areas," I said, repeating a comment Mal once made to me about the Huntsman.

"I don't see that we have a choice," Niall said. "However, there's a problem."

If the situation hadn't been so serious, I'd have rolled my eyes. "Of course there's a problem. This is Quest Investigations. When *isn't* there a problem?" I met Niall's gaze. "But solving them is our business, so what's *this* particular problem?" I blinked. "Do we have to find the horn in some kind of supernatural scavenger hunt?"

"Oh, we know exactly where it is. But retrieving it is… complicated."

I glanced between the three of them. "What aren't you telling me?"

"The horn is in the underworld forge." Eleri's fingers had sprouted thorns, and she'd snagged several holes in her leggings. "In the keeping of Govannon."

"The forge," I repeated stupidly. "The forge as in the supe high security prison?"

Niall nodded. "The very same." It was his turn to swallow. "I was a prisoner there for two centuries, and the only time I've been back since then was with Gareth. I'm sorry, but this time? I just…can't."

I wished I was confident enough to give Niall's shoulder a squeeze, but he was my boss and a Faerie prince. Even *I* wasn't that presumptuous. "That's fair. You can deputize us to go in your place."

Zeke dropped another spoon. "I can't either."

Eleri cocked her head. "Because the underworld is too much like Sheol?"

He shook his head. "No. That wouldn't bother me. Govannon isn't like the C-suite demons I used to serve. It's…one of the prisoners."

"Ah," Niall breathed. "Athaniel."

Zeke nodded. "My former AI. The angel interface that monitored me when I was on the Sheol work release program. I know he can't hurt me anymore. He might not even *be* in the forge at the moment."

"You mean he's *at large*?" I may have growled, because Athaniel was an asshole, and the idea of anyone hurting Zeke was un-freaking-acceptable.

Zeke held up his hands in a placating gesture. "No, not at all. The deal the C-suite demons struck with the supe council means he spends half the year laboring in Sheol and the other half in the forge. I just don't know where he is right now, and I…I can't risk facing him." He grimaced. "Sorry?"

Now Zeke I could comfort. I gave him a brief one-armed hug. "You don't have to apologize. You've got more than enough on your plate." I offered him a reassuring smile. "Still getting those prank calls?"

He chuckled weakly. "Unfortunately."

"Don't worry. Neither of you." I squared my shoulders. "Eleri and I will take care of it." Beside me, Eleri uttered a strangled squawk. I glanced at her, but she just grinned a bit forcedly. "Do I need special credentials to get in?"

Niall nodded, but the color was returning to his face. "I'll take care of it. I'll need to speak with my brother. It'll take a little time, but given the current crisis, he'll probably expedite the permits. In the meantime, you should get some rest. It's been a long and very eventful day." He glanced out the window where dawn was just beginning to glimmer. "And night." He gripped Eleri and me each by a shoulder. "Thank you. I appreciate you both more than I can say. I'll text you when it's time to meet back here to pick up your passes." He let go and took a deep breath. "I'd best get started, though. Delays at this point could be deadly." He strode out of the room.

"Well, *that* wasn't ominous," I said. There was a lot of that going around.

Zeke glanced between Eleri and me. "You're not mad at me, are you?"

"Not a bit," I said stoutly. "You're a rock star." I patted his shoulder. "So why don't you take off and spend a little quality time with *your* personal rock star. I'm sure Hamish will be happy to see you, and more than willing to offer snuggles." Or more. I had to tamp down a surge of envy. Not because I wanted Hamish—even though he was handsome, his high-energy approach to everything was way too much work. And not because I wanted Zeke, for whom I felt a much more brotherly affection.

Nope. It was way more pathetic than that. I wanted somebody to snuggle with myself. Someone who'd be there for me if I'd had a really bad day, or to talk things through with me if I was having a rough time figuring out...whatever. My approach to a case. My relationship to the supe community. Hell, what brand of peanut butter to buy.

I wanted a partner. And I wasn't likely to get one any time soon unless Wyn suddenly decided to come out from under whatever body of water he'd dove into to escape his homicidal ex. And I'm not referring to Lachlan. His *other* homicidal ex. Not that Lachlan was homicidal. Ugh. I rubbed my gritty eyes. I really needed some sleep.

"Eleri, I'll meet you at Ted's cave at seven tonight. That work for you?"

She hesitated for a second, but then nodded. "Sure. See you then."

I headed up to the fourth floor translocation door and used an FTA token to get home. I didn't specify Frang this time. I figured he needed a break as much as I did after our last off-road adventure. The driver who showed up was a dryad. I still had a tendency to flinch when faced with one I didn't know, but ever since Eleri and I had become friends, dryad hostility toward me had scaled way back.

This one was more subdued than usual, probably because gossip traveled faster in Faerie than a celebrity tweet, and she'd heard about the murder. She delivered me to Ted's cave mouth without a word. Which was probably just as well, because I wasn't feeling particularly chatty either.

I hiked down to my little rental house and fell onto my bed without even taking my sneakers off.

My dreams were full of drums. Pounding. Pounding. Pounding.

"Jeez," I groaned into my pillow, "at least work on that awful backbeat." As I blinked my bleary eyes, I realized that the pounding wasn't nightmare percussion. Somebody was hammering on my door.

I rolled out of bed and shambled through my living room. "Who is it?"

"Lachlan."

I jerked upright, running my tongue along my teeth and patting my hair. Ugh. I probably smelled like the underside of a derelict school bus and looked like I'd been living there. "Uh...I don't suppose you'd wait out there until I take a shower?"

His laugh rumbled. "Not a chance, lad. Let me in. You can clean up while I make you some dinner."

Dinner. My stomach growled. Dinner would probably be good. I threw the dead bolt and peeked outside. If my mouth hadn't been dry before, the sight of Lachlan Brodie with the sun picking out the light streaks in his shoulder-length brown hair, his shoulders broad enough to span the doorway, his scarred eyebrow quirked as he gave me a cocky smile, would have done the trick.

"Um. Hi."

He held up a battered cooler. "Let me in, Matthew. I've got mussels and fresh-caught salmon and the sooner we eat them, the better."

I held the door wide and let him in. He didn't kiss me—we still hadn't made it that far and if I were him, I wouldn't want to get anywhere close to me right now anyway—but his smile was as good as a caress. "The kitchen's that way."

"Hard to miss it." He glanced around the small living room. "Your place is a mite bigger than my boat, but not by much." He flapped one big hand at me. "Go make yourself pretty while I cook."

"Very funny," I grumbled.

He paused in the archway that led to the kitchen. "I wasn't joking." Then he winked.

CHAPTER TWELVE

I managed to make myself presentable and better smelling in less time than usual since I had a hot guy actually *cooking* for me in my kitchen. I'd heard somewhere that the best way to get a man's attention was to show up naked and bring food. I guess one out of two wasn't bad, when the person bringing the food looked as good as Lachlan did with his clothes *on*.

The path through my house was roughly circular—the living room led to the kitchen which led to the laundry room which led to the bathroom which led to the bedroom and back to the living room again. When I exited the bathroom in a cloud of steam, a towel around my waist, I could hear Lachlan humming something in the kitchen through my open bedroom door.

I was about to push the door closed so I could dress in privacy, but the sound of another person in my home was too unusual and exciting to shut out. Hadn't I just been wishing for somebody to be there for me?

"Hunh," I grunted as I opened the closet door, "I guess wishes do come true now and then." Although if *all* my wishes came true, Lachlan would be in here with me now and neither one of us would be wearing any clothes.

Later. After we solved this case, I'd do the smart thing and consult with Mal and Niall—and Lachlan—about the best way to find Wyn and set Lachlan free.

I sighed as I studied my unremarkable wardrobe. What do you wear for a trip to hell? Okay, so not hell as the fire-and-brimstone preachers would have it, but definitely a place that wasn't on Travelocity's top destinations list. I'd heard tales about Niall's time there. Not from him—he never talked about it. But from David who got it from Alun who got it from Mal who got it from Gareth.

Zero stars. Would not recommend.

Since I didn't have all that many style choices, I went with layering—T-shirt, jeans, sweatshirt that I could shed and tie around my waist since things were definitely toasty in the forge.

Toasty. "Ah, shoot," I muttered. Any artifact in the forge or Sheol could be hot enough to burn my hands, according to comments Zeke dropped from time to time. I needed insulated gloves if I didn't want my palms to blister. I glanced at the digital clock next to the bed. Just past five. I'd have time to pick up a pair before I met Eleri at seven as long as Lachlan and I didn't dawdle too much over dinner.

For now, I just grabbed the hoodie and tossed it on the sofa on my way through the living room to the kitchen. Lachlan was plating some truly delicious smelling fish—mmmm, butter and lemon—along with rice and green beans.

"This looks...wow." He'd already set a big bowl of steamed mussels in the center of my dining table. "Thank you."

"Have a seat. Beer okay for you?"

I nodded. "I can get it."

"Nay. You sit. You're due some looking after."

My throat *may* have gotten a little tight at that. Who was the last person who looked after me? I couldn't really remember. Well, there was Wanda at the diner, who refused to serve me any food she considered bad for me regardless of what I ordered, but she did that for all her customers. Zeke took care of the entire staff at the office. Ted's friendship had been warm but hadn't been this...this *personal.*

If this was what it was like to have a partner, I could seriously get used to it.

Lachlan smiled at me as he slid onto the wooden banquette across from me, the feast spread out between us. "You're looking a tad less rocky, lad."

"I feel less rocky." I inhaled the aromas of perfectly cooked fish. "I'll feel a lot better after I eat this, too. Thank you."

His smile was soft, without the edge or snark that he wielded like a harpoon at times. "My pleasure."

We ate in silence for a while—well, silence other than my moans of pleasure, because the fish was flaky and sweet and perfect, the mussels in their wine broth tender, the beans crisp. After I'd vacuumed up about half of mine, Lachlan said, "Are you ready to talk about it yet?"

I peered up at him. "Talk about what?"

"About whatever's got you strung tighter than a high test line." He held up a palm. "If it's a case, if it's confidential, I understand. But if you want to talk, I'm willing to listen."

Wow. Another wish come true. Had I rubbed a magic lamp without noticing? I toyed with a green bean. How much could I say? The murder of Sawyl was apparently an open secret in Faerie, but selkies weren't technically fae. My nerves were thrumming over the upcoming trip to the forge, though. Surely I could mention that without saying precisely why I was going. I'd count on forgiveness being easier than permission.

"I, um, have to make a business trip tonight."

Lachlan raised his left eyebrow, the one with the white scar bisecting it. "A business trip. Hopping on a plane, are you? Or is it a road trip sort of adventure?"

"Actually, Eleri and I are heading to Govannon's forge on an...errand."

Both his eyebrows snapped down. "You and Eleri? Alone?"

Even though I was nervous about it, I didn't care for the attitude that we weren't capable of accomplishing our mission. "Yes. Is that a problem?"

"Not as such," he said slowly, "but it could turn into one. I mislike you not having more backup."

"It'll be fine. We just need to ask Govannon for something. Soon as he gives it to us, we'll pop topside again. Piece of cake."

"Just ask a god for a little favor, is that it? Make a habit of that, do you?"

Since my current track record of asking supernatural beings for favors was less than stellar, I couldn't really fault Lachlan's skepticism. "No. But Mal's out of pocket, and there are reasons why it has to be Eleri and me rather than Niall or Zeke."

He nodded, a thoughtful expression puckering his forehead. "Aye, I can understand that. Both those lads have too much history to make the journey comfortable." He met my gaze squarely. "Are you all right with it?"

I nodded. "I am. From everything I've been told, Govannon isn't a smiting sort of god."

"All right then. You know your business best." He reached across the trestle table and gripped my hand. "But is it all right if I bide with you until you go?"

His fingers were warm against mine, the calluses on his palms a deliciously tender abrasion. "I— I'd like that," I said, my voice hoarse.

"All right then." He grinned and let go. "Finish up. I've got some lovely shortbread for pudding."

And though the shortbread was sweet, crumbly, and glorious, the loveliest part of the meal was the company.

After dinner, I washed the dishes—my house had a washer and dryer but no dishwasher, which was a tradeoff I could definitely live with—while Lachlan dried. Having someone Lachlan's size in my little house should have made me feel crowded, a little claustrophobic, but instead it felt...safe. Cozy. I warned myself not to get used to it, at least not yet.

"I need to head into town to pick up something for the trip," I told him over my shoulder as I headed into the living room. "Do you...want to come?"

"Aye. If you don't mind." He smiled at me again, but it was a little strained. Was he actually worried about me?

"Not a bit." I pulled on the hoodie and slipped into my jacket before slinging my camera bag over my shoulder. "You can leave your cooler here for now so you don't need to haul it around."

"My truck's outside. I can stash it there. But can I ask you something, lad?"

I paused by the front door, my hand on the knob. "Sure. What?"

"Why are you taking your camera to the underworld?"

I glanced down at the bag. "Habit, I suppose. It's been my job for my whole adult life. I see better through my lens."

"Think maybe you might come out from behind the camera now and again? See what the world looks like first hand?"

I frowned at him. "I don't hide behind my camera."

"No?"

I didn't. Did I? Whatever. I'd think about that later. "You can leave your truck here if you want. Stuff 'n' Things is only about half a mile away. I was planning to walk it since I'll be heading up to meet Eleri outside Ted's cave afterward." Heat rushed up my throat. *Ted.* I'd been in love with Ted for a couple of years before I'd met Lachlan. Somehow, it felt almost disloyal that I'd transferred my affections so quickly.

Well, transferring them *away* from Ted hadn't happened quickly. But transferring them onto Lachlan had taken no time at all. Furthermore, Lachlan knew exactly where Ted's cave was because it was where I'd broken trust with my bosses to give him a chance to get away from a potential murder charge.

But Lachlan clearly wasn't remembering that. Instead, he just looked perplexed. "Stuff 'n' Things? That's an actual place?"

"Seriously? You live on a boat on the Nehalem River and you've never gone to Stuff 'n' Things?"

Lachlan shrugged. "Our apartment was in Manzanita. We did all our shopping there."

"Well, you're in for a treat. Stuff 'n' Things is awesome. Between the store and Wanda's Diner, they're what makes Dewton the best place to live on the coast."

"I'll take your word for it, lad. Lead on."

We headed into town, Lachlan a warm presence at my side, his arm occasionally brushing mine. When we got to the sprawling store, its logo—*You need it? We got it.*—emblazoned in red above the front door, Lachlan paused to study it.

"Quite the claim."

I grinned. "Just wait. You'll be a believer by the time we leave."

We walked inside, through the vestibule and into the store proper with its mad jumble of…well, *stuff*, on sagging tables, eight-foot-high shelves, and in piles on the floor. Shirl, the owner, sat on her usual stool behind the counter, in her trademark jeans and red plaid flannel shirt, at least three pencils and a Sharpie shoved into her black beehive hairdo. She studied us from behind her cats-eye glasses.

"Matt," she said in her gravelly voice. Shirl sounded like a three-pack-a-day smoker, but I'd never seen her light up. In fact, she had *No Smoking* signs posted all over the store, even though it was a given with Oregon's Indoor Clean Air Act. "Who's your friend?"

"Shirl, this is Lachlan Brodie. He runs a charter service out of the bay."

"Hmmm," she said, then dismissed him and focused on me again. "Haven't seen you much lately."

"I've been busy at work. But I need a pair of leather gloves today. Heat proof."

She squinted at my hands. "Wait here." She ducked through the curtain behind the counter.

"Friendly sort," Lachlan muttered as he surveyed the eclectic contents of the store.

"Says the stroppy selkie," I murmured.

He gave me a warning glare. "Watch it, lad."

I gestured to the empty aisles. For some reason, whenever I came in here, I was always the only customer in the place. "Nobody around to hear, and if they did, they wouldn't think anything except *What does stroppy mean?*"

He huffed a laugh. "You may have a point."

Shirl emerged from the back room and slapped a pair of brown leather gauntlet-style gloves on the counter. "These'll do you." Then she carefully set a long box next to the gloves. "You got room in your bag for this?"

I gaped at the box. A Zeiss telephoto lens. "Shirl," I breathed as I lifted the lid and gazed at the lens lying in a nest of gray foam, "where did you get this?"

She shrugged one shoulder. "Same place I get all my stock."

I was tempted. *Really* tempted, because the lens was the next model up from my old one that was destroyed during the Great Dryad Debacle on the very day I'd met Lachlan. But I think I've mentioned that I can't mount just *any* lens on my bespelled camera.

So I sighed and I replaced the lid. "I wish I could, Shirl. But my camera has a…a special mount. This might not work."

She pushed it toward me. "Take it anyway and give it a try. No charge unless it works out for you. If not?" She shrugged again. "Bring it back and I'll find another home for it."

An interesting way to put things, and I wasn't one to resist temptation where my equipment was concerned. "You're sure?"

"Sure as I can be." She jerked her chin at my bag. "Get it stowed. I'll hold on to the box. Just in case."

"You're the best, Shirl," I said as I unzipped the bag and nestled the lens in the empty spot where the old lens had rested.

"I know," she said. Then she reached under the counter and pulled out something that looked like a post-modern lasso—a coil of braided yellow cord with a heavy carabiner dangling off one end. She glanced at it, nodded decisively, and then thrust it at Lachlan. "Here. You'll need this."

He accepted the coil, but it was obvious he'd only done it to be polite. "What's this?"

"Aramid cable. Titanium carabiner," she said.

"Aramid?" I fingered the cable. It was smaller in diameter than my little finger. Not as smooth as nylon or as rough as hemp. "Isn't that what Kevlar is made from?"

"Yes," Shirl said. "Kevlar's a brand name, but the material is the same."

Lachlan chuckled, but it sounded uneasy. "Granted a carabiner's always useful, but I prefer polypropylene or polyester cabling on the boat. Aramid doesn't knot well, and any shock load—like grappling with a great white—can damage it invisibly."

"G-Great white?" I croaked. "You run into *sharks*?" I'd seen *Jaws*. "You gotta get a bigger boat."

"Relax, lad. We selk—" Lachlan glanced sidelong at Shirl before giving me an overbright smile. "You needn't worry about that. I'm in no danger." He offered the cable to Shirl. "This is grand, ma'am, and I thank you. But it's a tad bit spendy for something that I've no real use for."

Shirl squinted at him, her eyes echoing the shape of her glasses frames. "Did you hear me quote a price?" She folded her arms. "On the house. If you don't need it, bring it back next week."

Lachlan's brows lowered, and I could tell he was about to argue. He had a thing about reciprocity. That's why he wouldn't sell the selkie crown jewels even when he needed money: In his mind, if he refused to take the throne, he wasn't entitled to the perks, even if the selkie clans insisted on practically forcing the bling on him.

On the other hand, I knew Shirl, and we really didn't have time for a stand-off. So I nudged his ribs with my elbow. "Resistance is futile."

He glanced down at me. "What?"

"Just take it. Like she says, you can always bring it back later. Or I'll return it for you."

He didn't give in right away—I could almost see the battle going on in his head from the expressions that flitted across his broad face. But then he shook his head. "All right, lad. For you."

"Exactly," Shirl rasped.

I didn't stop to decode that comment. Shirl was inscrutable at the best of times.

"Now shoo." Shirl batted Lachlan's hand away. "I've got inventory to wrassle with and it's past closing time."

I laid my hand on the small of Lachlan's back and pushed him toward the door. I'd tried pushing him before, so I was a little surprised that it was so much easier than I remembered. Hunh. Guess it made a difference when he actually wanted to move.

As we stepped out onto the sidewalk, the door lock clicked behind us. I glanced over my shoulder to see Shirl yank an old-fashioned window shade over the glass.

Lachlan stared down at the cable in his hand. "How does she know what I need?"

"I have no idea, but I've learned not to ask questions. She's never wrong."

Lachlan narrowed his eyes as he peered up at the Stuff 'n' Things sign. "Hmmm." Then he shook his head, his mane of hair flying in the breeze. "I wager there are stranger things in the world, like my boyfriend heading off to beard a god in his den." He fastened the coiled cable to a belt loop with the carabiner, making him look like a seafaring cowboy. "Best I learn to roll with it, eh?"

CHAPTER THIRTEEN

Boyfriend.

That word pinged around my brain all the way up the hill toward Ted's cave. Did Lachlan really think of me that way? Did I *want* him to think of me that way while he was still Wyn's *husband*, for Pete's sake?

Should I ask him about it? Talk about what he wanted? What *I* wanted? If I'd had the guts to tell Ted that I was interested in him—okay, that I was in love with him—before he registered with that matchmaking agency, would he have dated me instead of Quentin or Rusty? *Married* me instead of Quentin?

I snorted, only to have a Doug fir branch smack me in the face. A couple of months ago, I'd have suspected dryad intimidation tactics, but now I couldn't blame it on anything except inattention, which was pretty stupid on a dark trail.

Ted would never have married me because he was a grizzly shifter and I was human. We couldn't have had any kind of future because of the Secrecy Pact, and having your husband occasionally turn into a 700-pound bear—and not the kind you meet in gay bars—was a sure path to exposure. No, Ted and I would never have had a chance, even if I'd made my move sooner.

I glanced behind me. The path was narrow enough that Lachlan and I had to go single file. Weren't the same barriers that had existed between Ted and me also present between me and Lachlan? The only difference was that now I knew about the barriers. Eleri had told me once that selkies and humans were "a thing." Did that mean there were exceptions for relationships that traditionally crossed species lines?

I couldn't do anything about the whole supe vs. human scenario without more research and possibly special dispensation, but I could smash one barrier right now. All it would take was being honest about my feelings.

Crap.

We topped out into the clearing in front of Ted's cave. We were a little ahead of schedule, so Eleri hadn't arrived yet. *No time like the present.* If things got too awkward, I had a terrific excuse for bailing on the conversation: *Sorry, I'd love to talk, but I've got no time. I'm on my way to hell.*

Hell. Underworld. Sheol. The only thing that varied other than landscape was the degree of torment involved, and I was more than capable of manufacturing my own torment at the drop of a hat.

"So, Lachlan." I turned to face him in the center of the clearing. "Boyfriend?" Yeah, I'm *that* smooth. What can I say?

The scar in his eyebrow glimmered in the light from the rising moon, as though it were lit by some inner light. "Did you..." His gulp was audible in the quiet woods. "I'm sorry, Matthew. I thought you were... That is, that we..." He ran his big hands through his hair. "Ah, shite."

"Lachlan." I stepped closer and—shocker!—scared up the courage to rest my hand against his chest. "I'm really attracted to you."

He lost that shamefaced expression. "You are?"

"As you would say, aye. Do you... I assume you feel the same about me?"

His grin gleamed in the wan light. "Oh, aye." He peered down at me. "What's that look on your face?"

I immediately tried to look innocent—which, if you're wondering, is not a skill I've completely succeeded in mastering. "What look?" Yeah, like I said. Smooth.

"That look like you don't believe me."

My fingers twitched against his chest as I winced. "Man, I hope I have a better poker face when I interview clients and suspects or I'll *never* be a full-fledged investigator."

"The face you show to me—your *boyfriend*—isn't the face you show to others. I've noticed."

I snatched my hand away and shoved it in my sweatshirt pocket, folding my fingers as though I could keep the feel of him inside my fist. "You have?"

He nodded. "I notice everything about you." He captured my other hand and put it against his chest, his own warm palm holding it in place. I could feel his heart beating.

I couldn't meet his eyes, so I focused on his hand: big, broad, and scattered with tiny nicks and scars that spoke of his life on —and in—the sea. "You mean my ordinary face and ordinary hair and ordinary body that could stand to lose a good ten or twenty pounds?"

Before you think that it's only Lachlan who pings my odious comparison circuits, it's not. My self-confidence always takes a nosedive whenever I'm inching toward a new relationship. But, I mean, that's normal, right? Who ever thinks they're good enough for their partner?

And whoa—if you're about to cite examples, don't bother. I've heard them all, and even came up with a few myself. It just takes time to *believe* them, you know? Some insecurities are rooted really fricking deep.

Lachlan's chuckle sent vibrations from my palm down my arm to shiver in my chest. "Lad, I'm a selkie. My kind appreciates a little extra upholstery on our mates." He leaned closer. "Helps keep them warm when we take them for a jaunt in the ocean."

I blinked at him. "You *like* that I'm not ripped like…like…" I jerked my chin at his muscled torso.

"Matthew, you're exactly the right size and shape for you, so long as you're happy and healthy. You always will be, no matter what you weigh."

"Ah. Well." I cleared my throat. "Good then. I guess?"

"Very good. You know what else is good? You're exactly the right size and shape for *me*." His smile nearly turned my knees to water. "And you always will be."

Always. "That word has a different meaning for you than it does for me."

"It doesn't. You're loyal. You'd never stray. I know that as well as I know my own heart."

I huffed an exasperated breath. "I don't mean I'd change my mind or bail or *cheat*, for the love of Mike, but—"

"Who's Mike?"

I blinked at him. "What?"

"Who's this Mike bloke you're in love with?"

"Oh, for Pete's sake," I muttered.

"There's a Pete too?" Lachlan growled. "You only told me about Ted."

"There *is* only Ted. Or was, anyway. Mike and Pete—those are just sayings. My grandmother didn't approve of swearing. I picked up those phrases from her." I pointed at his nose. "But don't change the subject. What I mean is that *always* for supes is a much longer stretch of time than it is for humans. I'm almost thirty-seven, Lachlan—"

"Your birthday is coming?" he said, his expression brightening.

"Not the point," I ground out between clenched teeth.

"Then what *is* the point?" He sounded genuinely mystified, the big jerk.

"The *point*, Mr. Brodie, uncrowned king of the freaking selkies, is that I'm gonna get *old*. A lot faster than you. So my *always* and your *always* have entirely different time spans."

Lachlan rubbed the back of his neck. "Ah, lad. About that—"

"And why do you keep calling me lad? I'm thirty-six."

It was Lachlan's turn to blink. "It's naught but an endearment. I'll stop if you—"

"Sorry, sorry!" Eleri burst into the clearing in a swish of fir branches. "I had to stop by the office to get your pass for the forge and the formal request for the horn and Niall was late getting back from the council." She thrust a mass market-sized leather portfolio at me.

I took it and tucked it into my camera bag, wishing Eleri had been a tad bit later, because my conversation with Lachlan had just started to get interesting. "*My* pass? Don't you mean *our* pass? Or do you get an *automatic* pass because you're Welsh fae?"

She cast a nervous glance at Lachlan, who was looming at my shoulder. "The thing is…" She took a deep breath, and I noticed her hands were shaking like, well, leaves.

"Eleri?" I took a step toward her. "Are you all right? Did your clan chief pull another stick-up-his-ass move? Do you—"

"I can't go with you," she blurted.

Anger lit an ember in my chest. "So it *was* your clan chief. Seriously, if that guy doesn't—"

"No, no." She laughed, high-pitched and breathless. "He didn't forbid it or anything, probably because it's so far outside his imagination. I just…" She swallowed. "I don't do well around fire. It's a dryad thing."

I stared at her. "But you worked for a fire mage."

"Yeah, but his house wasn't literally *on fire*. Anyway, he was an asshole, so I could ignore his orders if I wanted. But Govannon is a god. One of *our* gods, our *elder* gods." She smiled weakly. "And *that* is a Welsh fae thing. So fire plus facing up to a god? I'm sorry, Hugh, but I just…can't." Her last word ended on a half-sob, which was so completely unlike the usually tough and unflappable Eleri that I knew she meant it.

I hugged her quickly. "It's okay. I understand." I let go and stepped back, patting my camera bag. "Will these credentials get me where I need to go? I mean, I'm still persona non grata in Faerie. I'm assuming that translates to a similar ban in the underworld."

"I'll go with you most of the way." She swiped a hand under her eyes. "There's an entrance to the forge through the Keep dungeons. I'll take you as far as the stairs." She bit her lip, and a couple of nearby Doug fir branches reached out to brush her shoulders as though the trees wanted to hug her too. "I'm really sorry, Hugh. I hate to send you there alone. I'll wait for you at the top of the stairs, as long as it takes, but—"

"I'll go."

Eleri and I both turned at Lachlan's matter-of-fact words. "What?" I said stupidly.

He gazed back at us, as calm and unruffled as if he'd just announced he'd grab us a couple of coffees from the break room. "I'll accompany Matthew to the forge. It's too chancy for a human to venture there alone." He shrugged. "So I'll go along."

Eleri's brow puckered. "But you're a *selkie*."

"Aye. Your point?"

Her frown deepened. "First, you're not actually fae."

"Close enough."

"Second, you're *water-based*. You're just as susceptible to damage by fire as I am. You might not burst into flames, but you could dry out until you're as desiccated as King Freaking Tut."

I turned to him, worry knotting my belly. "Lachlan? Is that true? Will you be in physical danger just by being there?"

I could swear his smile was fond as he gazed down at me. "We'll not be there long. And I'm in no more danger than you will be, although for different reasons." He gripped my shoulders and despite the speed with which this situation was devolving, I couldn't help leaning into his touch. "A human among gods and supe criminals." He shook his head. "Too risky by half. I'll not let you face it alone, lad. I'm going."

"Wow," Eleri breathed. "Talk about a grand gesture."

A boyfriend who'd go to hell with me? I'd never had a boyfriend who'd go to the *movies* with me if he didn't get to pick the film, so this was...different.

To tell you the truth, I wasn't sure how I felt about it. We hadn't even *kissed* yet.

Besides... "No. If it puts you in danger, I won't let you go."

He chuckled, his teeth glinting in the moonlight. "Lad, what gives you the least notion you could stop me?"

CHAPTER FOURTEEN

Eleri left us at the top of the darkest, steepest, *windiest* stone staircase I'd ever imagined, let alone seen. Because let's face it—giant rough-hewn stone castles featuring vast subterranean labyrinths lit with guttering torches aren't exactly thick on the ground in Oregon. Lachlan and I descended the stairs for what felt like hours, and I really didn't want to think what going back *up* those stairs would feel like. I hadn't spent nearly as much time on the StairMaster at the gym as I should have. Add to that the fact that the stair rise wasn't uniform—apparently Faerie didn't have the same building codes as the Outer World—and I was in serious cardio hell.

"I can't believe you came with me," I muttered for at least the fifth time since we'd started our descent. "This isn't what I'd call an ideal first date."

Lachlan had insisted on leading the way down the narrow stairs. He glanced over his shoulder at me. "We've spent time together before, including dinner not two hours ago. How are you counting this as a first date?"

"I'm not. Because it's a *lousy* date, just for future reference when you're planning, I don't know, an anniversary surprise or a romantic getaway." I steadied myself on the wall, the stone rough even through my leather gloves. Was it getting warmer? "Besides, dinner doesn't count because that was *before*. Before you announced I was your *boyfriend*."

He chuckled, the sound bouncing oddly in the stairwell. "Fancy a tumble on these stairs, do you?"

"What? No!"

"Nor do I. I told you I didn't trust myself alone with you, so dinner was a risk, but I wagered the food would occupy us. Leaving aside that next to a bloody great fire pit isn't the best place for snogging, we can't ask for a better chaperone than a god, eh, lad?"

"Lachlan, be serious. I never thought of myself as particularly high-maintenance. I'm too boring for that. But *this*?" I flung a hand out, indicating our less than romantic location. "*This* is way beyond the call of duty."

"I don't want you for just the good times, Matthew. Being a true partner, a true mate, means standing by each other in the bad times too." He paused two steps below me and turned so I could look directly into his eyes. "Like you did for me."

My belly fluttered like a startled bird. "Oh." Even though I'd barely breathed the word, it echoed in the stairwell as if I'd shouted, which made me flinch. "What is *with* these acoustics?"

He chuckled—which was as quiet as a breath—and headed back down the stairs. "It's Faerie, lad. It makes its own choices."

"Then I hope it'll choose to make this staircase shorter on the way up. Or maybe turn it into an escalator."

"Odder things have happened. I mind once when…" His steps slowed as a red-gold glow flickered against the massive stone blocks in the wall. Because of the tight curve, we couldn't see more than three or four steps ahead of us. "I believe we're about to enter the presence of a god."

"Good thing I wore my best jeans," I muttered.

Bravado, okay? My palms were sweating inside those gloves, even though they fit like, well, gloves. But you can't blame me. It's not every day you face a god, even if he happens to be a god who's pretty much abdicated. Zeke told me that these days, Govannon spent most of his time forging plumbing fittings for the Sheol renovation. Before, when Niall had been his prisoner, he'd done nothing but forge weapons all day only to melt them down again at night.

Another dozen steps and the stairs bottomed out in a small antechamber full of flickering light. It was large enough for Lachlan and me to stand abreast. The heat was intense, orders of magnitude greater than in the stairs, which made sense since the fires of Celtic creation were just beyond the stone archway.

Perspiration trickled down the back of my neck. Should I take the time to remove my hoodie? I probably should have done that before we'd started down the stairs, but the air in the dungeons had been dank and practically *breathed* eons-worth of cold.

But then I glanced at Lachlan, and my discomfort seemed trivial. I might be sweating, but he was…drying out. His lips, usually so full and soft-looking—not that I'd had a chance for more personal exploration yet—were already rough and cracked. His face wasn't ruddy so much as flat-out reddened, as if he'd sustained a massive sunburn or was about to succumb to heat stroke.

I squeezed his hand, and though I cursed the gloves that kept me from feeling his skin, I was grateful to Shirl for the way they protected my hands from the heat: If my hands were burned, I couldn't do my job, and if I couldn't do my job, more than Lachlan's and my temporary personal discomfort could be at stake.

"Let's get this done so we can go home."

He nodded, not even a hint of regret in his resolute expression. "Let's."

We walked through the archway shoulder to—well, not shoulder, because he's at least a foot taller than I am. Shoulder to biceps. Really, *really* impressive biceps which at the moment were hard as rocks from the way he was clenching his fists.

I don't know what I expected from the forge. Maybe something a little more rustic? It looked more like the hot shop in that glass-blowing competition show, assuming the fire wasn't contained inside a dozen furnaces, but blazing right there at the front of the room.

I'd known Govannon was big, but clearly my concept of scale was way off. I mean, Lachlan was tall, but the smith god was *gigantic*, more than twice Lachlan's height, his broad back in proportion, and his arms as massive as you'd expect from someone who spent all day, every day, since the beginning of time swinging a hammer as big as I was.

I'm not joking. That thing was literally six feet long, and the clang it made as it struck the enormous anvil was deafening.

The prisoner who was working the bellows—I was relieved to note he was wearing ear protection and gloves along with his FDOC coverall—looked furious. And familiar. With a shock, I realized that the man fanning the flames, as it were, his silver hair flopping over his sweaty forehead, was none other than Pierce Martinson, former fire mage, and the man I'd helped consign here not three months ago.

And another prisoner—my size, coloring, and general shape —who was lugging a load of scrap metal across the cavern, was his son Reid, the necromancer wannabe who'd planned to murder Lachlan to ignite his own power.

Yeah, the vicious glances shooting our way from both of them probably weren't just generic *You're free and I'm stuck in this damn prison* looks. They were personal, because if it weren't for Lachlan and me, they'd still be prancing around upstairs as their rich, entitled, asshole selves.

The guy who was just disappearing down a corridor hauling an armful of completed pipes was also someone I recognized: Patrick Lassiter, who'd tried to murder his nephew and ended up nearly taking out the entire supe community with a misplaced curse. It was Quest who'd put him down here too.

Any minute, Zeke's old tormenter Athaniel could show up as well, so, yeah. We needed to move this visit along before the prisoners staged a riot and tossed us into the flames.

I pulled out my credentials, but then stood for a moment, nonplussed. How the heck could I attract Govannon's attention? His hammer swings were so regular and forceful. I could hardly go up and tug on his loincloth and say, "Excuse me, but could I have a minute of your time?"

Luckily, Lachlan was made of sterner stuff—or else he had more experience interacting with random gods than I did. He took my arm and towed me to Govannon's side opposite from Pierce Martinson and just enough in front of the anvil so that we caught the smith's eye.

He set down his hammer and turned to Pierce. "You may take a respite. All of you."

With one last venomous glance at us, Pierce and Reid scuttled down the hallway where Patrick had disappeared. Govannon looked down at us.

"It is not every day I'm visited by two so ill-suited to my realm," he rumbled in a voice like distant thunder. "What is your business?"

I presented my pass and the formal request from the council, although given our proximity to the fire, I half expected the parchment to burst into flames. Apparently the council had bespelled it to withstand the heat, though, because it stayed clean and crisp as Govannon took it between his massive thumb and forefinger.

His bushy eyebrows, a good twelve feet overhead, lifted. "Herne's horn, is it? Eons pass with no one asking, and now two requests in less than a year."

"Two requests?" I asked, my investigator instincts firing.

"Aye, although the first was my own offering, you ken? But that the horn is needed again? Betrayal." He shook his massive head. "It is not honorable."

"No," I agreed. "That's kind of its definition."

He focused his gaze on me with eyes that were bigger than my head. The flames of the fire were reflected in their dark depths—unless the flames were actually dancing in his eyes, which I suppose could be possible. "I've never entertained a human. Not a full human." He tilted his head and reached out a finger until it paused a hand-span from my chest. I tried to hold my ground and not flinch. "May I?"

Lachlan shifted uneasily next to me, and I could almost feel his knee-jerk *hell, no* reaction, but who were either of us to deny a god? I nodded.

Govannon's touch was surprisingly gentle. "Ah. Not so different, after all. I'd forgotten. I've not ventured into the Upper World since..." He retracted his finger. "Never mind." He glanced at Lachlan, who, once I wrested my attention from Govannon, I could see was swaying on his feet. "Best get you both on your way."

He straightened, and it might have been my imagination, but he seemed to get even taller. He lifted an arm, stretching it high, and without looking reached for a spot on the wall over his head. His fingers brushed the stone and he frowned. He peered upward, and I was right—he *could* get taller, because suddenly his eyes were on the level where his hand had touched the wall. He peered at it, his nose almost touching the stone, and patted the area within his arm span, which by now was at least forty feet.

He took a step back, the ground trembling with the weight of his tread. He returned the parchment to me. "I fear I will not be able to meet the council's request."

"B-but why not?" I accepted the decree, which looked no bigger than a postage stamp in his enormous hand. "The paperwork is in order. All the seals intact."

"It is."

"Please, sir...your worship...your godliness—"

"Govannon will do," he said in a somber rumble. "I'm no god of yours. No god of anyone's anymore."

I blotted the sweat off my forehead with my sleeve. "It's vital that we speak with Herne. A person has been murdered, and—"

"I understand," Govannon said. "But I still cannot comply."

"But—"

"Lad," Lachlan rasped, "I think what he's trying to say is he can't hand over the horn because he hasn't got it." He gazed up at Govannon, who'd shrunk to his original humongosity. "Isn't that so?"

Govannon nodded. "Herne's horn," he said, "that has been in my keeping these many millennia, is missing."

CHAPTER
FIFTEEN

"I don't get it," I complained as we sat around the conference table at the Quest offices. Thankfully, Faerie had taken pity on us and the stairs back up to the Keep had been three ordinary flights, tops. Eleri had been waiting for us as promised, and handed us each about a gallon of water. Now, we were both more or less back to normal. "How could Govannon not notice the horn was missing?"

Niall hadn't stopped staring at the table over his steepled fingers since we'd given him the news. "The horn isn't ordinarily visible. It only manifests when someone reaches for it."

"So if somebody knew where to reach, they could waltz into the forge and pluck it off the wall anytime they wanted?"

Niall lifted his brooding gaze from the table and speared me with a *Seriously?* glare. "The forge isn't someplace you just *waltz into*. Aside from the fact that it's—"

"Uncomfortable as all blazes," Lachlan muttered. He still looked a bit parched. I hustled over to the conference room's mini-fridge and grabbed a couple more bottles of water for him. He smiled at me sweetly when I set them in front of him. "Thank you, lad."

"Really wish you'd stop calling me that," I murmured. "I'm not a kid."

He winked at me. "That I know, trust me."

"As I was *saying*," Niall said with a wry, knowing smile, "entering the forge requires permission from someone in authority. If you don't have it, you can't get in."

"*You* did," Jordan piped up. When we got back, he'd been waiting at the office with Doop in tow. The hound was currently stretched out under the table, gnawing on a Frisbee. "When you and Gareth snuck into Faerie to keep the Convergence from going kablooie."

Niall narrowed his eyes. "How do you know that?"

"*Everybody* knows that," Jordan said, reaching for a scone from the coffee service plate. I noticed he passed half of it to Doop, who accepted it with remarkable delicacy for something with jaws that big.

"*I* didn't," I said.

"Oh." Jordan passed the other half of the scone to Doop and took another for himself. "Well, everybody at the Dog House then."

Niall just shook his head and sighed. "Werewolves and their bloody boundary issues." He met my gaze. "There were several reasons Gareth and I could get in. First, he's a bard, the only one, and as such gets a pass pretty much anywhere. Second, we took an…unconventional route, one that has since been warded by Bryce." He grinned. "Not for any security consideration, mind, but because he objects to the potential impact on"—he tapped his lower lip—"how did he put it? Ah, yes. *A fragile, irrecoverable ecosystem, you asshole.*"

Lachlan set down his second empty bottle. "Is there a third reason?" By his tone, he already knew the answer, and by Niall's glare, he knew that he knew.

The two of them engaged in a stare down for about thirty seconds, before Niall caved, although I suspected his capitulation was more for the Quest team than because he was intimidated by Lachlan. He *was* the King's brother, after all.

"Yes, you bloody selkie. It was because I'd been a prisoner there myself." His glare faded. "Getting in wasn't a problem then. Getting out—well, that's the other reason I didn't want to make this trip. Without Gareth, a bard, or my brother, the current authority for the forge prison, along to vouch for me, I'd have risked getting chucked back on the chain gang." His smile was twisted. "Two hundred years of that was enough for getting on with, thanks."

I couldn't hide my wince. Compared to what Niall had gone through in his unfair captivity and Zeke's thousand plus years of slavery to his demon overlords, my shorter human lifespan didn't seem quite as much of a drawback. At least I had less time to endure pain—even if it was unrequited love (Ted), chronic uncertainty/blue balls (Lachlan), or wishing for what I couldn't have (supernatural heritage).

Yeah, compared to them, I had it easy. You'll note, however, that doesn't stop me from griping about any and all of it. Sue me. I'm only human.

"Let's get back to the main question, shall we?" My tone might have been a little sharp, judging from the startled looks everybody shot me. You can't blame them—I was usually the last person to take charge in our meetings. "What happened to the horn?"

Niall's brows drew together. "The last I saw of it was when Peadar turned it over to me after Herne dealt with Rodric Luchullain and...and Tiarnach." Niall cleared his throat on that last word. Tiarnach was the former Unseelie King, the one who'd condemned him to that stint in the forge. He was also Niall's father, so discussing his death at the hands—and jaws—of the Wild Hunt, no matter how deserved, probably pushed a few buttons for him. "I tucked it into a mini-portal and it disappeared, presumably to return to its usual place."

"So you didn't actually see it there?" I asked.

He shook his head. "I haven't been back myself. But remember, even if I had, I wouldn't be able to see it unless I reached for it."

I frowned, tapping my pen on my notepad. "Does it manifest because of location or because of the intent of the reacher?"

Niall's eyebrows shot up and he blinked twice. "I...don't know. Perhaps both? Govannon seemed to know where to grab for it, although I imagine whatever spell holds it in place would involve keeping it above the heads of everyone except the person who's supposed to guard it."

"In other words, Govannon." I sketched the rough floor plan of the forge as I remembered it—the arch where Lachlan and I had entered, the fire pit, the hallways leading off the main cavern, the anvil. I stared at it for a minute. "I wonder if the spell was specific to him or to his size."

"What do you mean, lad?"

I gave Lachlan the stink-eye at his use of *lad*, but he just winked again. "Look." I drew a rough—very rough—elevation as seen from the entrance, with Govannon sized more or less as we'd first seen him. I flipped the pad up so everyone could see.

"What's that supposed to be?" Jordan asked, dusting scone crumbs off his hands. I checked the plate—they were all gone and Doop was licking his chops.

"What's what supposed to be?"

"That." He pointed at my Govannon sketch—okay, so it was a stick figure. I told you it was rough!

"That's Govannon."

"Oh. I thought it was a basketball hoop." He screwed up his face in what I'd come to recognize as his apologetic expression. "Sorry, Hugh. It's a really cool drawing."

Eleri snorted, and Niall hid an obvious smile behind his hand.

"My *point*," I said, teeth gritted, "is that the caster might not have keyed the spell to Govannon personally, like a...a biometric. Because they didn't have to." I drew a Pierce Martinson stick figure next to the anvil, and if I gave him horns, who could blame me? "See the size difference? The other prisoners are ordinary human-sized." I glanced at Niall. "The same as you. So no need to get fancy with the spell."

Zeke leaned forward, frowning at my drawing, but more as though he were considering my words than judging my artistic ability. "Keying the spell to a single individual is more complicated and time consuming. Also, from my observations, some of the oldest spells are the simplest because the casters operated from a set of basic assumptions rather than considering all possible scenarios."

Niall huffed, sliding forward in his chair in a defeated posture that was more suited to me. "That's all well and good, but it still should have worked. There's nobody Govannon's size, not in the forge or out of it." He frowned thoughtfully. "Other than Prometheus, but his context would be Hades, not the forge. He'd never show up in the Celtic underworld."

I remembered my introduction to the supernatural world, when Ted's husband Quentin went full-on jealous incubus on my ass. "They wouldn't have to be tall," I said slowly. "Not if they had wings." Everyone goggled at me. It was like being in an aquarium full of really good-looking fish. I glanced at Zeke apologetically. "Athaniel has wings."

"B-but..." Zeke had gone as pale as the cream in the coffee service. "Athaniel's wings are hobbled. It's part of his sentence. He can't fly."

I leaned forward, sure I was on the right track. "We didn't see him, although I suppose that doesn't mean he wasn't there. You said he spends half his incarceration in Sheol, right? Do you know when?"

"I'm not sure."

"Somebody would have to come get him, right? And some demons have wings. AJ does. So does Quentin."

"They'd never have stolen the horn," Zeke said, scandalized.

"I know that. But if two demons have wings, surely others do too. Like that dude who showed up to arrest Athaniel at Bryce's place."

"Paimon? Why would he need the horn?"

I clutched my hair, as close to exasperated with Zeke as I'd ever been. "Not him per se, either. But if whoever came to escort Athaniel to Sheol had wings, they could have taken the horn. Does Govannon ever sleep?"

Niall shook his head. "No. But he's occasionally out of the cavern for other reasons."

I lifted an eyebrow. "Like to confer with the Sheol escort, for instance? How many demons are we talking about there, anyway?"

"Three," Zeke said immediately. "Two guards and a supervisor." He rolled his eyes. "There's *always* a supervisor."

"I bet the supervisor is the one ordinarily chatting up Govannon. So if one of the guards has wings—"

"They could have taken the horn, even if they had to paw around for a while to grab it," Eleri said. "Good job, Hugh."

Jordan raised his hand tentatively. "Excuse me, but there are other prisoners. Wouldn't one of them have said something?"

Eleri patted his arm. "Oh, you sweet summer child. You think any of the prisoners would lift a finger to aid their jailers? Snitching wouldn't help *them*, so if I know the Martinsons, they'd jump at the chance to stick it to the man." She smirked. "Or god, in this case."

"Pretty sure Patrick Lassiter couldn't give a rat's ass about maintaining the status quo," I said. "Probably in those guys' opinions, anything that disrupts the forge would be a bonus."

Jordan reached under the table to scratch Doop's neck ruff, and although the dog's eyes went half-lidded in pleasure, I suspected the action was more for Jordan's comfort. "Why would they want to call Herne and the pack then? If they were plotting a prison break or something, calling Herne wouldn't help. He'd be more likely to chase *them*. Wouldn't he?"

Eleri topped up her coffee. "All of them consider their incarceration unfair. Maybe they wanted to sic Herne on the council as a way to appeal their sentences."

"They're all terminally narcissistic," Niall said, "but even Athaniel is canny enough to know that could backfire in a major way. Herne's not bound by written laws. He's more in tune with the infinite, I suppose you could say. Although if he murdered Sawyl before he went on the lam, he might be throwing in his lot with them for some other reason."

Doop snuffled at my sneakers, and something niggled at the back of my brain. Grizel and her laundry. The abandoned kennels. The missing horn. *That's it.*

"They didn't take the horn because *they* want to call Herne." Excitement practically sparked out my ears. "Don't you get it? They took it so *nobody else* could call him."

I looked from Niall to Eleri. From Zeke to Lachlan. From Jordan to, well, Jordan. "They can't afford for the *Cwn Annwn* to be at full strength. For the Wild Hunt to ride. For Herne to sic the pack on their rightful prey. Because *they're* the rightful prey."

Niall's jaw sagged in shock. "Danu's tits," he croaked.

"What?" Jordan glanced wildly from me to Niall. "What?"

I met his eyes squarely. "It's a conspiracy, Jordan. Somebody's planning a massive betrayal, and if we don't figure out who, what, when, where, and how, we could be looking at a revolution. And if that happens, no world—not Faerie, not Sheol, not the Upper-Outer-Wider-Whatever human plane—is safe."

"Do you think Herne is dead?" Jordan asked in a small voice. "Grizel had his clothes after all."

I drummed my fingers on the table. "If he were, they wouldn't need the horn. Anyway, Herne's like a god, right? How do you kill a god?"

Niall waggled his hand. "He's not a god. More a...force of nature. Supe muscle, if you will."

"A minion." Zeke was still pale. "Someone who performs tasks for an overlord."

Niall gripped Zeke's shoulder, for comfort probably. The two of them were close because their boyfriends were in the same band and they traveled to concerts together all the time. "You're not a minion anymore, mate, and you won't be ever again. But Herne doesn't answer to an overlord. When the Hunt rides, he can pursue anyone who falls within his definition of traitor, conspirator, or oath-breaker."

"I'll wager these blokes are all three," Lachlan drawled. "But if Herne's not dead, where have they stashed him?" He glanced under the table. "Him and the whole pack of *Cwn Annwn*. They couldn't very well have slaughtered the lot without someone noticing." Jordan whimpered, and Lachlan had the grace to look contrite. "Sorry, laddie, but it had to be said."

I watched Zeke retrieve a soft-bristled whisk out of a pocket dimension to brush scone crumbs off the table. "Sheol," I said. "That's where they put them all, in one of those pocket dimensions. If demons took them, that would only make sense."

Zeke paled even further, and I hadn't thought that was possible. Any more and he'd disappear altogether. "But if that's so, they'll be impossible to find. The Realm Accords specify that all Sheol's alternate dimensions must be decommissioned and newly licensed, but the work isn't anywhere close to done. There were hundreds of the things, maybe thousands."

I scowled at my drawing. "So we look in all of them. Go door to door."

He shook his head. "It's not like there's a map, Hugh, and no single C-suite demon knows all the locations. They...distribute knowledge, so none of them has to do all the work. And if one of them is in on the conspiracy, they'd never give us directions, anyway."

I glanced under the table, where Doop had abandoned the Frisbee—which looked more like neon green plastic lace by now —and was gnawing happily on Herne's jerkin. "We don't need directions. We've got something better." I grinned, jerking my thumb in Doop's direction. "We've got a hellhound."

CHAPTER
SIXTEEN

The next few hours were absolute chaos. Niall had raced off
to let the council know what we feared and what we planned.
Mal was staying with them to act as liaison and, along with his
brother Alun, as a last line of defense should the suspected
conspiracy succeed before we had a chance to A) find out what
it was in the first place or B) stop it by any means necessary.
And Niall said that the council was adamant about that last bit.

No methods were off the table when it came to preventing a
supocalypse.

Anything—and I mean *anything*—that we deemed necessary
was copacetic with them. Considering Niall O'Tierney, the
Unseelie Court's legendary bad boy, was heading up the team,
anything covered a pretty wide range of mayhem. The council
must be serious about this.

Well, it was a serious thing. I mean jauntering off to *another*
hell—and really, one should be my limit in any given lifetime,
let alone any given day—wasn't exactly something to take
lightly. All of us had shifted into a battle mode that I didn't
know we possessed.

Well, I knew Niall and Eleri possessed battle modes—I'd seen
them, and in Eleri's case, had been on the opposite side a couple
of times. Lachlan had one I'd witnessed too, but he'd
disappeared from the conference room—now referred to as the
War Room—while I was rooting around in my office looking for

the spare memory card for my camera. Bryce was going to try to cobble together a quick and dirty heat resistance spell to keep my equipment from melting. Despite Lachlan's snark about me hiding behind my lenses, no way was I visiting Sheol and not documenting the experience.

Besides, we had no idea whether we'd find what we needed in this trip. Reviewing the photographic evidence might be the only way we could locate Herne and the pack.

Assuming they were still alive.

I wasn't entirely confident that absconding with Herne's clothing before Grizel had a chance to finish her laundry meant that he wasn't already dead. Even if he'd been alive when they'd transferred Athaniel and taken the horn—which, Zeke had discovered through some judicious snooping, had happened at the equinox—that didn't mean they hadn't killed him since then. Zeke had told me stories about Sheol. It wasn't exactly the most salubrious environment, even after the upgrades that Rusty Johnson and his company had instigated after the Realm Accords. For one thing, demon overlords had a tendency to forget their charges needed food and water.

After retrieving the newly heat resistant memory cards from Bryce, I walked back into the War Room to find Niall and Zeke arguing, although Zeke never stopped prepping our go-bags and Niall never stopped checking the alarming number of bladed weapons he had secreted about his person. I really hoped those were heat resistant too, or he was going to have a lot of interestingly shaped burns when we got back, some—I winced as he tucked a knife into the back of his leather pants—in very inconvenient places.

"I'm going," Zeke said, his jaw tight and his face blotchy red, although this time it appeared to be from anger, not embarrassment. "End of story."

"Absolutely not. Hamish would kill me if something happened to you—not that I'd blame him." Niall was *not* using his inside voice. "And then Gareth would kill Hamish and Tiff would kill Gareth and Alun and Mal would get involved and that doesn't bear *thinking* about."

"Gentlemen," I murmured, "you can't fight in here. This is the War Room."

They both glared at me. "What are you talking about?" Niall barked.

I plopped my camera bag on the table. "Really, you supes need to work on your human cultural references if you expect to keep passing unnoticed. After we're done with this case, we're having a movie night, and *Dr. Strangelove* is first on the list." I glanced from Zeke's clenched jaw to Niall's thunderous frown. "What seems to be the problem?" I asked mildly.

"Zeke wants to go with us."

"I *am* going with you."

"I *told* you," Niall roared, "that idea—"

"Is actually pretty good," I said.

Niall rounded on me. "You stay out of this. You're know nothing about it. You're—"

"Human?" My teeth were on display, but make no mistake: I wasn't smiling.

Niall pushed off from the table where he'd been leaning to bellow at Zeke. "Shite," he muttered. "That's not what I... Look." He glanced from my camera bag to the packs Zeke had prepped for me, Niall, and presumably himself. "If it were up to me, none of you would be going. You're my staff. You're my *friends*. I can't put you in danger this way."

Zeke hugged one of his ubiquitous silver space blankets to his chest—although what we'd need blankets for in Sheol beat the hell out of me. "Do you think I can stand watching you all walk into that same danger? None of you has ever been to Sheol. You've had minimal interaction with demons, and trust me when I say that AJ and I are *not* typical, especially not of the C-suite executives or even middle management. You don't know how they operate. I do. You *need* me on this mission, Niall." He lifted his chin. "Furthermore, you *know* you do." He glanced over his shoulder furtively. "Although don't mention it to Hamish. He won't take it well."

"Exactly!" Niall said, punctuating his words by jabbing a finger toward Zeke. "And he *has* been to Sheol."

"And almost screwed everything up, so don't use him as a model, okay?" Zeke's expression changed to one of entreaty. "Please, Niall. Let me help. The Upper World—*this* world—is my world too now. I don't want anything to happen to it."

Niall deflated then. I'd learned that about him over the last year. He was all about the swagger and bravado—he and Mal both were—but let one of us sincerely ask for their help and they turned into puddles of super-handsome fae goo.

I was double checking my camera bag when Lachlan walked in with that damn leather rucksack of his, Shirl's cable attached to a strap on one side. I eyed the bag suspiciously.

"Is your skin in there?"

He chuckled as he slung it on the table with all the other baggage. "Nay. The witches' collective put the security spells back on my boat, so I don't have to lug it around with me anymore."

I poked at it with one finger. It still looked just as full as when it had held his skin. Also just as lumpy. "If you can leave your skin, why are you still carting the selkie crown jewels around?"

I'd never imagined Lachlan Brodie could look *cagey*—he was way too direct for that—but there was no other way to describe his expression. "Lachlan." I loaded my tone with warning. "What's in the bag? And what are you doing here anyway?"

His jaw did that granite impression again. "You're going to Sheol. I'm going too."

"*Seriously?*" I glared at him. "You nearly passed out at the forge and we were only there for a few minutes. We have no idea how long we'll be searching through Sheol dimensional pockets for Herne. You're *water-based*." I moved closer to the big, strong man who had haunted my dreams lately—replacing the big, strong man who'd haunted them for the previous two years. "You can't go. It's too dangerous."

"I've got that covered." He opened the pack and pulled out a bundle of fabric as silvery as Zeke's space blankets. He shook it out and held it up for me to see.

I stared at it, nonplussed. "I've heard of tinfoil hats, but a tinfoil overcoat?"

He scoffed. "Nay. A bespelled duster. Bought it off Ronnie Purl."

"Oh, *that's* a ringing endorsement. He's a ferret shifter who can't keep his mitts off things that don't belong to him. What makes you think this is anything but a glorified gum wrapper?"

"Ronnie may have sticky fingers, but he knows quality when he sees it. I had the collective double check the spells for me, if that eases your mind a trifle. Hold it for me?" I took it from him while he shrugged out of his anorak. He lifted that damn scarred eyebrow at me.

"Yeah, yeah," I muttered and held up the coat like a bargain basement valet so he could slide his arms into it.

"It'll keep me cool and undesiccated for at least twenty-four hours," he said as he turned around, the silver fabric flaring out behind him. "That should be plenty of time." He bent his head to fasten the buttons.

"How do you know? We have no idea how long we'll be there."

"Because if Niall O'Tierney lets any of you—even yon demon receptionist—remain longer than that, I'll have his head on a pike. Although"—he frowned when the top buttons wouldn't close over his massive chest—"I'll not have to make the cut since he won't last more than a day there either."

"Comforting," I said dryly. "Do you suppose your chill suit will do its job, Mr. Seal, considering you can't, er, seal it?"

His gaze was hot enough to make me think we'd already made the jump to Sheol. "I don't care. You're human, Matthew." I still shivered when he pronounced my name that way—

MattHugh—as though he saw and accepted both sides of me. "A human in Sheol with his soul still attached? It's never been done. And I don't trust those demon blighters to toe the line."

My heart tried to leap up my throat. *I guess he's serious about this boyfriend thing.* My voice was a little hoarse when I said, "Yeah. Zeke doesn't trust them either. That's why he's insisting on coming along."

Both Lachlan's eyebrows rose this time, halfway to his widow's peak. "Your demon's going along? Is that wise? Other than you, he's the one most vulnerable, being as they bent him to their will from the time they conjured him into being."

"He's got a reason to resist now that he's got Hamish and all of us. But he's the best person to advise us on how to deal with the overlords, so he does have a point. Speaking of which…" I jabbed a finger at the pack. "Don't think I didn't notice that you dodged the question. What're all those lumps in your pack?"

He sighed, further straining his magical overcoat, and reached into the pack to pull out—

My eyes nearly bugged out. "Holy crap! That ruby's as big as my fist. What the heck are you doing carting it around? To *Sheol*, for Pete's sake?"

Lachlan tucked it back in the pack. "Insurance."

"Insurance?"

He fussed with the buckle on the pocket for a little longer than necessary before he straightened to face me again. "As I said, I don't trust them, Matthew. If the overlords try to pull a fast one with you or Zeke or even O'Tierney, I need something to hand to bargain with." He shrugged. "I figured Sheol, you know. Fire. Heat. They'll probably prefer rubies to emeralds or sapphires." He patted the bag. "Although I brought a few of those, just in case."

"Lachlan." My voice broke on his name, because seriously, this man? He may not have Ted's sunny disposition and eternal optimism, but he had a heart as big as the ocean. "You told me you'd never touch these because they were payment for a job you wouldn't take."

He rested his hands on my shoulders, his grip warm and gentle. "Lad, you're worth whatever sacrifice I have to make, whatever debt I have to pay." He grimaced. "Don't get me wrong. I'd rather we all got out of this as slick as a dolphin's leap."

"But better to be safe than sorry?" I gazed up at him. Dammit, I couldn't let this go without a kiss. His chin was tilted down toward me. If I lifted on my toes just a little bit, I could—

"Brodie," Niall barked, striding in with Zeke at his heels, "I should have known you'd show up."

Argh. My co-workers had the *worst* timing in all the worlds. On the other hand... I stepped back from Lachlan and busied myself with my camera bag. It was probably better if we kept things strictly G-rated until Lachlan was finally free.

I just hoped I wouldn't be pushing ninety by the time that happened.

CHAPTER SEVENTEEN

Since Bryce adamantly refused to let us open another Sheol-access pit in his wetlands, he'd collaborated with the local witches' collective and the other druids in his circle to set up a portal in one of the Quest workrooms.

This one was on the third floor, not far from my office, and knowing that opening a portal into literal hell was possible not thirty feet from where I booted up my computer every day wasn't precisely comforting. I mean, yeah, I dug all the supernatural stuff, but I preferred my coffee without a side of brimstone, thanks.

Even though I'd been working for Quest for over a year, I'd never ventured farther into any of the workrooms than their doorways. Mal and Niall had claimed it was for my own protection. Apparently, humans were...ingredients in some now-illegal spells, and though the rooms had presumably been cleansed since then, my bosses didn't want to take chances. Which, yeah, I was totally on board with that. Becoming the accidental equivalent of eye of newt or toe of frog wasn't exactly on my bucket list.

But I trusted Bryce MacLeod completely, and if he said this portal spell would be safe for me, it'd be safe.

That didn't mean I went charging into the room, though. I paused in the doorway, Lachlan hovering at my shoulder, and peeked inside. Bryce was conferring with a witch in Maiden aspect who was apparently dialing into a modern college student vibe—skinny jeans, slouchy sweater, ankle boots—rather than the floaty chiffon outfit that I'd seen on the magistra who'd attended Ted's trial. For all I knew, this one *was* a college student. Now that Bryce's druid side was awakened and he had the ability to detect auras, he could instantly spot the supe students at the college where he taught.

Zeke was all but plastered to the wall just inside the door, his jaw set but his knuckles white as he clutched his own pack to his chest. I edged into the room to stand next to him.

"Do you know what our destination is?" I asked.

He nodded. "The nexus cavern underneath Portland. It's where Hamish"—he gulped, but followed the nervous tell with a dreamy smile—"negotiated for me."

"So mixed feelings?"

Another nod. "You could say that. But it's the closest anchor point, so it makes sense."

"Anchor point?" My fingers twitched with the urge to pull out my notebook. "What's an anchor point?"

Zeke turned to me with an almost relieved expression, as though he was grateful for something to take his mind off his imminent return to his original realm, which wasn't exactly home, sweet home. "Dimensional manipulation is tricky. Unless you've got a physical construct to act as an anchor, it can be highly unstable."

The light dawned, and I *really* wanted my notebook. "Like St. Stupid's?"

"Exactly," he said. "Because United Memorial has such a massive physical footprint, the dimensional architects are able to create...well...not *unlimited* space for St. Stupid's, but certainly as much as the supe community has ever needed, even during the Hrodgar's Syndrome crisis."

"But Sheol's different?"

He winced a little at the word *Sheol*, but who could blame him? "Yes. Or at least it was. The overlords could expand the realm at will by spawning dimensional pockets at slightly different frequencies. Sort of"—he sketched a rough sphere with one hand—"reusing the same space. It gave them unlimited control over Sheol's capacity, but it was also a major weakness."

I'd heard about that little caper. It was tied up with one of my first cases with Quest and ended with Zeke's boyfriend Hamish nearly bringing Sheol down with his relentless repetition of the drum solo from "Wipe Out."

"I take it the overlords learned from past experience?" Lachlan asked dryly.

Zeke blushed. "You could say that. When Mr. Johnson started renovations, he designated several anchor points that had to be strictly physical. Alternate dimensional pockets had to be tied directly to those foundations, and therefore generally accessible as well as stable. It's part of the new licensing regulations."

"I'll wager that got a few demon drawers in a right twist," Lachlan murmured with a chuckle, his duster tinkling like wind chimes with his movement. "Haven't met a laird yet who took kindly to having his domain diminished."

"Oh, no!" Zeke said brightly. "It actually worked out well for the C-Suite. They're making a killing repackaging the free-floating pockets and selling them in the secondary market." He chuckled. "Now that soul collecting is severely restricted, they're discovering the joys of capitalism for increasing their wealth."

I frowned. "Wait. You mean Quest's pocket dimensions—including the one that houses our *secure cloud storage*—used to be part of *Sheol*?"

Zeke tilted his head, his brows bunched in confusion. "Where did you think they came from?"

"I thought they were, you know, *new*. Constructed for purpose."

"You mean like demons?" Zeke's tone was wry, but anger swirled in my chest on his behalf.

The jerks with the most power in Sheol used to manifest new demons whenever they needed a minion to do their dirty work, and they made certain the new guys on the block couldn't do anything *except* that dirty work. Zeke's friend AJ, for instance, was manifested to tend his progenitor's library, so he couldn't handle fire, like, at all. Not even a controlled flame on a stove. On the other hand, he could read at super speed, could understand all written languages *ever*, and remembered everything. He also had three extra pairs of arms, the better to carry stacks of books, although mostly he kept those tucked away in the ether.

"Man," I muttered, "some people claim the internet is the tool of the devil, but our IT infrastructure has actually *been* a tool of the devil. Or at least devil-adjacent." With a grimace, I peered at Zeke from under my brows. "I don't suppose we could request pristine space? A dimensional pocket that hasn't been refurbished?"

Zeke shook his head apologetically. "By the terms of the Realm Accords, they're not allowed to create more, only repurpose what they've got."

"So they'll run out eventually? What then?"

"The renovations won't be completed for quite a while," Zeke said, "especially since Mr. Johnson has to fit them in around his other jobs, and there were *a lot* of alternate frequencies. But I heard the C-Suite demon in charge of business development is considering shifting to a subscription model."

"Talk about hellish," I grumbled.

"If you'll excuse me," Zeke said, "I need to fetch Doop." He trotted out of the room.

Niall beckoned to me from the east cardinal point where he stood next to a wrist-thick black candle atop a wrought iron stand that looked like it had come directly from Govannon's forge. I joined him, Lachlan sticking to my side like foil-wrapped beefcake. Eleri, who was assisting Bryce, caught my eye. From the way her shoulders shook, she was trying not to laugh. I frowned at her. Spells required precision—heck, even I, clueless human that I was, knew that much—and if she didn't focus properly, we could end up in the middle of the lava river instead of the nexus cavern.

Bryce exchanged one final low-voiced word with the witch and then strode over to us. His dark hair was sticking up in all directions, a sure sign that he'd been clutching it regularly during the spell prep. His dark eyes were intense and serious. "We're set." He glanced at each of us in turn, his gaze resting longest on me. "If you're all sure about this."

Niall nodded. "It's our best shot."

"We've configured the portal spell to...Sheolify your possessions when you step through, so they shouldn't experience significant degradation for at least twenty-four hours." Bryce handed Lachlan, Niall, and me a pair of safety glasses that wouldn't have been out of place in my college chem lab. "These are spelled to allow you to see in Sheol's limited light." I started to put mine on, but Bryce blocked my hand. "*Don't* put them on until you pass the portal. If you wear them in Upper World light, you might sear your retinas."

I gulped. "Good to know." I pointed to the last pair in his hand. "Is that an extra set? In case one of ours breaks or we lose them?"

He glanced at the glasses as if he'd forgotten he held them. "No. I didn't realize Eleri wasn't going until after I'd already made all four." He tucked them into one of the many pockets on his tactical vest. "I'll save them, although with luck, we'll never need to make this kind of trip again."

Niall frowned, looking around. "Where's Zeke?"

"Um..." I scanned the room too, although the whole slate-floored, slate-walled, slate-*ceilinged* space was bare of furniture or any other hiding place. "He left to fetch Doop. I thought they'd be back by now."

"We don't have time to waste," Niall said. "I'll go—"

"Hi, everybody!" Jordan said brightly, almost skipping into the room with Doop prancing along at his side, a much less battered Frisbee clamped between his teeth.

"Jordan?" If Niall had said my name in that tone, I'd have headed for the nearest MAX stop. "What are you doing here?"

Zeke slunk in behind Jordan, Herne's very much worse for wear jerkin hanging limp in his hand. "I'm sorry, Niall. But Doop wouldn't come with me. He'll only follow Jordan."

"Danu's tits." This time Niall was the one who clutched his hair, although it didn't have the same mad-scientist result as when Bryce did the same. "I can't take *Jordan* to *Sheol.*"

I half expected Jordan to fall back on his beseeching sad-puppy-eyes look, but instead, he stepped up and faced Niall, his jaw set in a stubborn line I'd never seen before on the happy-go-lucky werewolf. "Can you command Doop? Will he listen to you? Can you *protect* him?"

Niall huffed, although whether with exasperation or helplessness, I couldn't tell. "I can't promise to protect *anybody.* This whole venture has disaster written all over it, but *not* proceeding could be worse."

"I know I'm a screw-up," Jordan said evenly, "but I'm Doop's best shot at making it back unhurt, and your best shot at convincing him to do what you want. Whatever this conspiracy is, it threatens *my* world too." He straightened his shoulders, and suddenly he looked fully adult. "Am I a Quest employee?"

"You're an *intern*," Niall said, clearly at the end of his not-very-long rope.

Jordan didn't back down. "Does that mean no? Or yes? I mean, I get a paycheck, same as Hugh and Zeke and Eleri." He wrinkled his nose, dropping back into his familiar puppyish guise for an instant. "I'm sure it's not as much and we don't talk about that anyway, because it would be unprofessional. But am I part of the team?"

Niall hesitated, and I could see him wrestling with what was good for the mission versus what was good for Jordan—although I was beginning to think the two were the same.

"Bryce *does* have an extra pair of Sheol-vision goggles," I murmured.

Niall shot me a *We'll be talking about this later* look before he finally nodded. "All right. But I'm running this show, even though Zeke's taking point once we get on site. You—" He pointed at Jordan's nose, causing him to go nearly cross-eyed. "—will hang back, keeping Doop on a *very* short leash, until we're ready for him to track Herne. Get it?"

Jordan nodded eagerly. "Got it."

"Good." Niall took a deep breath and faced Bryce. "All right, my brother. Send us to hell."

CHAPTER EIGHTEEN

Stepping through the portal into Sheol was like...well, I wasn't sure exactly how to describe it. I'd heard tales of what it had been like before the Realm Accords, and much was still the same: hot, dark without our special goggles—I checked—a vague rotten egg smell, and did I mention hot? But the shrieks of the tormented that Hamish had described in far too much detail were absent.

The nexus cavern was vast, the stalactites on its ceiling barely visible high up amid the gathered shadows. A dozen or so openings gaped in its blackened stone walls, and weirdly enough, each cave mouth had a sign over it in multiple languages, including what looked like hieroglyphics, like the directory in an office building or department store.

"Those signs are new," Zeke murmured. Unlike the rest of us, he'd taken his glasses *off*. It was the first time I'd seen him without them, and he looked...vulnerable. "Rusty installed them as part of the Realm Accords renovations."

I squinted at the nearest one. The English translation read: *Break Room 437, Dorm Wing 3B176A, Inhuman Resources, Customer Service (Closed)*. "Jeez," I muttered, "how big is this place?"

"As big as it needs to be," Zeke responded grimly. "And sometimes bigger. Which is the problem we have to solve."

"Right." I gingerly opened my camera bag in case the anti-heat spells weren't as robust as Bryce claimed. "Pocket dimensions."

"Exactly." Zeke shuffled over to a spot in roughly the center of the space, his toes inches from a blackened area on the stone floor. "This is where Hamish's drum kit stood when he came to get me. Mr. Johnson returned it when he and his crews cleared the rubble from this cavern, but it was too fire damaged to repair." He wrapped his arms across his stomach as if he were cold, although *that* was patently impossible. "I think the demons Hamish tricked took out their frustration on the drums, although they couldn't completely destroy them because of Bryce's protection spells."

I joined him and squeezed his shoulder. "Is this the first time you've been back?"

He nodded. "Yes. It's not..." He blinked rapidly and cleared his throat. "I knew intellectually that the population had decreased since the Realm Accords. Some of the demons who can function in the Upper World have opted to relocate, and all the contracted souls are being released as their cases are reviewed." He shot me an apologetic glance, as if Sheol's former conditions were somehow his fault. "They're not needed to stoke the boilers anymore since Rusty switched to geothermal energy."

"Swell," I said, studying another sign: *Lava Pools, Shackle Storage, VIP Lounge (Under Construction)*. If I were one of those souls, I'd want out of here *tout de suite*, especially if I'd been cooling my heels—or heating them, as the case may be—for centuries already.

"But I didn't realize it would feel so...so *empty*."

Niall strode over to us, a scowl pinching his brow. "Hugh, be sure to document everything. If we can't locate Herne this time, we may need to come back, and the more information we have about the layout, the better."

"Right." I crouched down and set my camera bag on the rough stone in front of me, the go-bag Zeke had prepped for me bumping on my back. When I lifted my camera out of its padded compartment, it still had the wide-angle lens mounted on it. I studied the telephoto lens from Stuff 'n' Things. Did I dare use it? It would make it easier to capture the detail of the cavern's entrances and signage without having to hike around the perimeter, which, in a place this big, could seriously cut into our time.

I decided to risk it and switched out the lens. I looped the camera strap around my neck, shouldered the bag again, and stood. Everyone else was quiet as I snapped shot after shot. Even Doop was subdued, dropping his Frisbee at Jordan's feet and sighing.

"Okay," I said at last. "I think I've got enough. Now what?"

Zeke turned in a circle, clearly at a loss. "I'm not sure where to go. Things are so different."

Jordan pointed to one cave. "That sign says *Reception*. Why not start there?"

The rest of us shared a shamefaced glance. We were clearly in an alternate dimension if Jordan was the only one talking sense.

But we dutifully trooped into the dark cave maw, Zeke in the lead, followed by Niall, and then Jordan and Doop. The dog had retrieved his Frisbee, although his tail was tucked between his legs.

Lachlan was attempting to have our six like a big, foil-wrapped caboose. I slowed down until I could walk next to him. "You doing okay? Your chill suit doing its job?" Perspiration was beaded along his hairline, but he didn't look as...as *beached* as he had at the forge.

He smiled at me rather grimly. "Grand."

"Uh huh. Tell me another."

He squeezed my elbow. "Truly. I'm all right. You're looking a mite overheated though."

Yeah, understatement. While Lachlan was merely glowing with a sheen of perspiration highlighting all his good points like he was under the lights at a glamour photoshoot, I was approaching flop sweat territory. Zeke had warned us to wear long sleeves and pants despite the heat, because there were other things, from rocks to corrosive fumes, that could damage our skin. But at the moment, I was wishing for a tank top and cargo shorts with every heated step. "I'll live."

I winced. Until I'd started at Quest—especially on the last couple of cases—I'd never realized exactly how many catch phrases and euphemisms involved variations on *life* and *death*. I needed to be careful down here: The souls still awaiting their day in court might have certain *feelings* about those terms, particularly since *life* wouldn't be an option for them, regardless of the outcome of their case review.

I glanced around furtively. Were any of them lurking around here? What did souls look like? I should have been grateful for the shiver down my spine, but what can I tell you? I'm a man of many contradictions.

Ahead of us, Zeke stopped, staring at the wall. As we got closer, I saw that it wasn't a wall—it was a door. A door that looked like it had been lifted straight out of a 1940s noir detective movie, with its frosted glass upper panel lettered in gold: *Reception and Disposal.*

"Well, *that's* not disturbing," I muttered. "It didn't mention anything about disposal on the sign back there."

"I guess they've got you coming and going," Lachlan said with a chuckle.

"Now is not the time for jokes," I murmured out of the side of my mouth.

"On the contrary, lad, now is the best time. We need all the morale boosts we can manage."

Zeke glanced over his shoulder. "He's right. Fear is one of the overlords' chief weapons. If we rob them of that—"

"We disarm them?" I asked.

Niall patted Zeke's shoulder. "Lead on, then. We're with you."

He nodded and stepped inside.

If the door looked like something out of a Sam Spade movie, the room behind it could have been lifted straight out of *His Girl Friday*. Behind a waist-high wooden counter was a bullpen's worth of desks with clattering manual typewriters and shrilling old-style black desk phones. Of course, the typewriters were clattering without benefit of actual typists, and who the heck would be calling hell on a landline?

"Seriously?" I muttered, looking around. "Rusty renovated the place to look like it needs another renovation?"

Zeke shrugged. "The demons in charge of each department got to pick their design motif. I believe Naberius, the one in charge of soul intake, is a big film buff. Also a little stage-struck." He nodded at the line of black and white head shots along one wall—actors from stage and screen going back literally centuries, if the photos of Edmund Kean, Sarah Bernhardt, and Charlie Chaplin were any indication.

Jordan was squinting at the desk closest to the counter. "Do you hear that?"

"Hear what?" Niall asked.

Jordan pointed to the desk's phone, its handset floating in the air. "That's Zeke's voice."

"What?" Zeke squawked.

"The message on our voice-mail. Can't you hear it?"

All of us crowded next to Jordan and leaned over the counter. With all the noise in the room, it was impossible to detect anything. How had Jordan— *Oh*. Right. Werewolves didn't only have a heightened sense of smell. They had enhanced hearing, too.

Just then, there was a brief lull in the clacking and ringing, and Zeke's voice was clearly audible, tinny and faint. "You've reached Quest Investigations."

The rest of the message was lost when the noise increased again and the handset clattered back in its cradle. We exchanged wide-eyed looks.

"Holy crap," I croaked. "Those hang-up calls were coming from *hell*?"

"Wow," Jordan said. "I guess I owe my cousins an apology. Or I would if I'd ever accused them, which I didn't. Although I probably should have, huh?"

"Never mind." I patted Jordan's arm as I glanced around the noisy yet unpopulated office. "How do you suppose we get somebody's attention?"

"There's a bell on the counter." Jordan pointed to one of those old-fashioned dome-shaped concierge bells. "Maybe we should ring it?" Without waiting for a response from any of us, he reached out and tapped the button briskly several times.

Immediately, a frazzled-looking person in a scarlet cassock burst out of the door in the far corner, their attenuated arms waving in agitation. "Stop that at once! Don't you realize—" Their oversized eyes widened. "Ozul-y-Kalon."

"Who?" Jordan asked.

"That's Zeke's true name," I whispered to him. "Forget you've heard it."

Zeke, to his credit, didn't cringe. "Vepar. We've come seeking information."

Vepar tugged at their Peter Pan collar. "You're from the auditors?"

Zeke glanced sidelong at Niall. "Auditors?"

"The *auditors*. About the missing funds." Vepar clutched their wispy white hair. "They promised to give us time to track down the perpetrators. Another week, at the very least. We can't be expected—"

"We're not from the auditors," Niall said soothingly. "But we would like to speak to someone about a possible unsanctioned visit."

Vepar eyed us all. "You mean other than yours?"

Niall coughed into his hand. "An *involuntary* visit. To be more precise, a kidnapping." He leaned casually against the counter. "And since the Realm Accords passed, that sort of thing is frowned on." He smiled affably. "As are the people who abet such outrages by not sharing the appropriate information."

Vepar glared at Niall irritably. "Fine. Wait here." They practically sprinted for the door, their cassock billowing like a sail, and slammed the door behind them.

"Touchy sort," Lachlan said.

Zeke sighed. "You have no idea."

"How long do you suppose they'll keep us waiting?" Jordan said. From the way he was shifting from foot to foot, I guessed he hadn't visited the restroom before we left, and there was a dearth of trees in Sheol for convenient leg lifts.

"As long as they want," Zeke replied. He glanced at the narrow space where we stood between the counter and the door. It was a tad overfull of *us*, but contained no chairs. "Make yourselves as comfortable as possible, I guess."

"In the meantime," Niall said, "we should probably decide what questions we want answered, although I'd suggest we start with finding out who's in charge of escorting Athaniel from the forge."

Jordan sidled over to Zeke. "Is there a, um, restroom?"

Zeke bit his lip, obviously holding in a smile. "I believe I saw a sign in the corridor."

When Jordan reached for the door, Niall caught his arm. "I don't want any of us going anywhere alone."

"I'm not alone." Jordan's expression was definitely pained. "I've got Doop with me."

"That's not what I—"

"I'll go along with the laddie," Lachlan said. "I saw that sign too."

"Thank you, Brodie," Niall said.

"No thanks necessary." He held the door for Jordan and Doop to precede him, then closed it after himself.

I sighed. Guess I couldn't even pass the time flirting. I leaned against the counter and checked my camera. Still plenty of room on the memory card. I scrolled through the pictures I'd snapped in the nexus cavern, humming in pleasure at the new lens's resolution. Telephoto shots could be grainy, but these were unusually clear. I could make out every—

I frowned, squinting at the photo of a tunnel mouth labeled *Sauna, Payroll, Ice & Vending (Out of Order)*, one of the last I'd taken. There was some kind of distortion right in the middle of the shot. Could the lens be degrading, either because of Sheol's conditions or because of the council's camera spells?

I lifted the camera to my eye and peered through the viewfinder.

And nearly fell over backwards. Because those empty desks and levitating phones and clattering typewriters? They weren't just stage props. Every one of them was populated and in use.

But the workers were only visible through my brand new telephoto lens.

CHAPTER NINETEEN

"Uh, guys?" I croaked. "Could you take a look at this, please?"

Zeke stopped chewing on his lip and staring at the closed door. "Hugh? Are you all right?" Leave it to Zeke to worry about everybody else when he had to be experiencing some extremely uncomfortable deja vu.

I pointed my camera at the desk farthest from the counter, where, according to what I could see through the lens, a gaunt woman dressed like a Victorian suffragette, complete with a *Votes for Women* sash, was jabbing at a manual typewriter with extreme prejudice.

Frowning, Niall peered through the viewfinder. "The desk? Is there something odd about it? Other than the disembodied typing?"

"You don't see her?"

His eyebrows rose. "See who?"

"Zeke." I practically thrust the camera in his face. "You see her, right?"

Zeke leaned in, but not too close, obviously compensating for glasses that weren't there. "I'm sorry, Hugh. Perhaps if you told us what you want us to look at?"

I started to hyperventilate. This wasn't some Sheol-induced hallucination, was it? Something that Bryce hadn't anticipated? Jaw clenched, I pressed the shutter release, and the instant the click sounded—perfectly audible despite the ambient noise—the woman's gaze shot from her typewriter to me. Her expression was…not friendly.

I ignored it for the moment and checked the LCD display. She showed up there, like one of the transparent waltzers in the Disney Haunted Mansion ride. I flipped the camera toward Niall and Zeke. "Please tell me you see her now."

Their identical looks of shock would have been comical if panic wasn't still trying to scale my ribcage.

"A soul," Zeke breathed.

"Souls are here? Now? *Invisible?*" I squawked.

"Not invisible so much as incorporeal," Zeke replied.

"Invisible, incorporeal, insubstantial. Whatever you call it, they're still incarcerated. What are they doing here? I thought the Realm Accords were supposed to send everybody"—I made a rolling motion with one hand—"onward."

"It's on a case-by-case basis, remember, subject to review. And as I understand it, there's quite a backlog at the review tribunal." Zeke shrugged. "Apparently there's a staffing shortage."

"Yeah," I muttered, "and management is handling it by putting the souls of people who ought to be free back to work." I dared another peek through the viewfinder. "*Awp!*" My Victorian suffragette was standing right in front of me, glaring daggers—and she'd brought friends.

All the people—*souls*—that I'd seen through the lens had abandoned their desks and were clustered on the other side of the counter. All the typewriters had gone silent, and though the phones still jangled with incoming calls, no receivers were floating in the air anymore. My finger spasmed, and I took another shot inadvertently, which really ticked off the crowd. "Sorry! Sorry!" I was babbling, but who cared? "Didn't mean to disturb you. Putting the lens cap back on now."

When I tried to replace it, though, my hand was shaking so much that I dropped it and it rolled under a hinged pass-through to the other side of the counter. I was debating whether I ought to run now and ask questions later when the cap rose in the air and floated jerkily toward me, as if it was in an invisible someone's hand. I glanced at Zeke, who made a *go on, take it* motion.

So I plucked the cap out of the air. "Thank you." This time I managed to affix it to the lens without dropping it. The phantom spiders that liked to stage kicklines up my spine had arrived, though. Were all those souls still staring at me? Were they angry at me? What did they want? And furthermore...

"Why can I see them through the lens but you two can't?" I murmured.

Zeke tilted his head, considering. "I'm not entirely sure. But perhaps because these are human souls and you're human?"

"But then why could you see them in the photo?"

"If Zeke's right," Niall said, "then perhaps visibility requires a human conduit—such as your action in taking the picture. Where did you get that lens?"

I wasn't sure whether Shirl would get in trouble with the supe council for inadvertently selling magical artifacts, so I hedged. "At a second-hand store in Dewton."

Niall lifted a brow—he could tell I was holding something back—but simply extended his hand. "Could I see your camera, please?"

I glanced at the spot where Victorian Suffragette had stood. "I'm not sure they're okay with being impromptu models."

Niall turned away from me and bowed to the room. "I mean no disrespect. But I believe it may be important for us to conduct an experiment."

No incorporeal being chucked a typewriter at Niall's head, so that was a good sign. In fact, at a couple of desks, the clack of keys started up again, although Victorian Suffragette's machine was still silent.

I handed Niall the camera. He removed the lens cap, setting it carefully on the counter with a wry glance in my direction. He pointed the camera toward the active typewriters, one by one, and clicked the shutter release. He studied the screen, expressionless, then turned the camera to show Zeke and me.

The shots showed only the empty desks.

"Apparently," he said, his tone dry, "the lens's...enhanced capabilities are keyed to you. It may respond similarly to any human. However, without exposing the community, we can't exactly test that hypothesis."

I wasn't sure whether to be elated or terrified. For the first time since I'd discovered that supes were real, being human was actually an advantage. But would this paint a bigger target on my back? And did the lens only work in Sheol? So many questions, and I had no idea how to begin to find answers.

Just then, Vepar yanked the door open so hard it banged into the wall. They paused just inside the room and glared around. "What are you doing? Stop gawking and get back to work. The Auditor General could be here *any minute*."

Typewriters started clacking again, telephone rotary dials spinning, and handsets floating. I'd never imagined that typing could sound disgruntled, but then, I'd never been to Sheol before.

Vepar marched over to us. "A supervisor will arrive to escort you to Customer Service."

"But the sign said Customer Service was closed," I blurted. I was grateful for Bryce's heat resistance spells, because Vepar's glare could have legit set me on fire.

Did you know typewriters could snicker? Yeah, me either, but I could swear they did.

"Special circumstances," Vepar hissed. "But I must ask you to return to the nexus cavern and await him there. You are a disruptive influence"—they glared at Zeke—"and we have *so* much to do."

"Of course," Niall said smoothly, his hand on Zeke's shoulder. "When should we expect the supervisor?"

Vepar glowered at Niall. "When he gets there. And if the Auditor General arrives while you're waiting, for Lucifer's sake, *don't speak to him.*" They hustled back into their office and slammed the door.

"Zeke," I murmured, "can Vepar see the souls?"

Zeke sighed heavily. "I expect so."

"Then why can't you? You're a demon too."

"But I was only a low-level minion. I was never rated for soul-collection until Melchom wanted to punish me by making me contract for Hamish's." He spread his hands, palms up. "Since it wasn't necessary for me to see souls, my progenitor didn't build that ability into me when I was manifested."

"Purpose-built people," I muttered. "Talk about revolting eugenics." But to banish that devastated look from Zeke's face, I patted him on the back. "The joke was on Melchom, though. You collected Hamish's heart instead."

Zeke smiled and ducked his head, blushing. "We should probably go before Vepar takes it out on everyone here. We can wait for Jordan and Lachlan in the corridor."

When we stepped out the door, Jordan, Doop, and Lachlan were just returning, Doop's white fur gleaming as bright as Lachlan's silver duster in the gloomy hallway. The dog still held his Frisbee clamped in his jaws, and didn't seem at all bothered to be relegated to collar and leash.

"How is that thing not melting?" I said, pointing to the Frisbee. "It's hot enough in here to turn it into Silly Putty."

Jordan glanced down at Doop. "Dr. MacLeod said the portal would Sheolify our possessions. Maybe it worked on the Frisbee too, since it's Doop's possession."

"Really?" Niall said, his tone laced with disbelief. "You actually surrendered one of your prize Frisbees to a dog?"

Jordan lifted his chin. "It's *his.* I bought it for him special." He patted Doop's head. "But I'd share my stash with him, too. It's the *responsible* thing to do."

Responsible? I wasn't sure. But kind? Absolutely. Jordan was definitely growing up.

"Come on. Let's get back to the nexus cavern," I said, studying Lachlan's ruddy cheeks in the dimness. Was their color the result of overheating, or just his general robust good health? While my vision through the Sheol-goggles was okay, I wouldn't call it sharp. "The sooner we confer with the supervisor, the sooner we can get out of here."

Once again, Lachlan brought up the rear as we trooped down the hall. But as we emerged into the vast cavern, I felt something tugging at the back of my jeans. When I glanced over my shoulder, Lachlan was hooking the carabiner from Shirl's cable to my belt.

"Lachlan, what the heck? I'm not Doop, and if this is the kind of kink you're into—"

"Take it easy, lad. This is just a precaution." He gazed down into my eyes. "When yon werewolf and I were heading for the loo, it was almost impossible to keep him in sight, even though he was no more than a few feet from me, and wasn't trying to run away. These spectacles"—he tapped his goggles—"may let us see, but Sheol isn't a place used to giving up its secrets." He grinned crookedly. "Humor me in this? I don't want to lose you."

Well, when he put it like *that*...

"All right." I pointed at his nose. "But don't get any ideas about pulling the same thing upstairs. I don't mind protectiveness, but controlling behavior? That's a deal-breaker."

His grin grew brighter. "I'll make a note of that."

When we joined the others, Niall raised an eyebrow at my new accessory, but surprised me by saying, "Good idea." He scanned the cavern, scowling. "Something's going on here that raises my hackles."

"Doop's too," Jordan said. "Look."

The hound had dropped his Frisbee and was tugging at his leash, snuffling at the ground, the fur on his spine standing straight up.

There was something about that spot...

I lifted my camera and scrolled through the shots, past Victorian Suffragette, to the photo that had made me want to test the lens in the office in the first place: the one with the anomaly.

I studied the picture, glancing from it to Doop and back again. "Guys, I think Doop might be on to something." I held up the camera. "I caught this weird distortion in the air right there. I thought it was a problem with the lens but now I'm not so sure."

Something moved in the corridor beyond the dog.

"Doop!" Jordan's shout made me lose my grip on the camera and it banged against my chest. The dog had yanked his leash out of Jordan's hand as he'd lunged forward. It was trailing along the stony floor, practically at my feet, so I grabbed for it. I looped it around my fist just as Doop took a flying leap, hauling me through the air behind him to land...

Somewhere else.

CHAPTER TWENTY

I stumbled when I landed, losing my grip on the leash as I grabbed for my camera. I managed to stay on my feet, just barely. Doop whined and pressed against my legs.

"Easy, boy," I murmured as I looked around. Whereas the nexus cavern had looked like exactly that—a giant cave where multiple tunnels converged—the place where Doop had dragged me looked more like the vestibule leading to a warehouse or storage facility. Concrete floor, cinderblock walls, zero ambience. It was a tiny room—maybe eight by ten at the most, so it was damn good luck I hadn't slammed into the opposite wall when we made our less than graceful entrance, although I had banged my elbow as I caught my balance.

"Pocket dimension, I presume?" I said, just as one of the concrete blocks in the corner shed a trail of rubble. Judging by the piles of similar detritus that lined the pock-marked walls, this pocket dimension could use some serious TLC.

Gooseflesh rose on my arms. Doop and I were in another dimension that seemed unstable, and I didn't want to hang around and see how long it would take to collapse. Unfortunately, the wall we'd burst through was completely blank—no door, no window, nothing. Nothing except...

"Lachlan's cable!" The carabiner was still attached to my belt, but the cable looked as though it was extruded from the middle of one block. If Lachlan was still holding on to the other end, he could pull us out.

I tugged lightly on the cable, just a signal that I was here. I couldn't remember how long it was, but apparently there was a lot of slack because my tug met no resistance. I pulled on it some more, hand over hand, but not too fast. I didn't want to yank it out of Lachlan's hands. Coil after coil fell at my feet. "How long *is* this thing?"

Suddenly, I was holding the end of the cable. I stared at it stupidly for a minute, shivering. Our only lifeline to the outside and I'd screwed it up. I fought down a sob, since it wouldn't do a damn bit of good. I took a deep, steadying breath and turned around, paying closer attention to the little room.

No windows, no doors, but the right-hand wall had a gap like the opening for a heating duct with a remarkably straight line of dust across its threshold. I crouched down and peered inside.

It was a tunnel, about ten feet long and square-walled, with light—or at least the Sheol equivalent of light—at the other end. I glanced at Doop, who was still plastered to my side. "What do you think, boy? Should we check it out?"

He dove into the tunnel, although he had to creep along practically on his belly. "Guess that answers my question."

I tucked my camera back in its bag while I waited for him to clear the passage. Then I crawled in myself, scattering dust as I pushed my camera bag in front of me. The go-bag on my back scraped along the ceiling. "Next time," I muttered, "I'm wearing kneepads."

I continued to shiver as I made my way through the tunnel, and suddenly I realized that it wasn't from shock or fear—or at least not entirely. The temperature had dropped significantly from the nexus cavern and seemed to dip further the farther along the tunnel I crept.

"Why is it so freaking *cold* in here? This is Sheol, for Pete's sake." My breath clouded in front of my face as I reached the end of the tunnel. I poked my head out, directly into Doop's furry flank. "Damn it, Doop, move."

But the hound was shivering too, and I realized Jordan was right: He *was* cold, as in refrigerator level cold. "What the heck?" I shoved at him, scooting him along the concrete floor in a scrape of toenails until I could emerge from the tunnel and stand up.

"Holy crap," I breathed.

If the room where we'd landed looked like a warehouse vestibule, this was the warehouse, the concrete and cinderblock motif extending into a space maybe thirty by fifty, with a rusting corrugated metal roof high overhead.

But the place felt smaller than that because it was teeming with white-furred, red-eared hounds, all of them bigger and fiercer-looking than Doop.

"Guess we found the pack, huh, Doop?" He just shivered harder and huddled against me. I wondered about that—they were his companions, weren't they? Presumably his mom and dad were in here someplace. But then I looked closer. The pack —at least two dozen dogs—weren't just milling around. They were pacing, panting, their eyes showing white.

They were terrified.

Then, along the side wall, something rose from beneath them, like the bare, forked branches of a dead tree. My fingers clenched in Doop's ruff, seeking comfort. I didn't have the best relationship with trees, depending on the mood of nearby dryads. Was there such a thing as a dryad demon? Would it be angry at being disturbed? Had all umpteen *Cwn Annwn* lifted their legs on it, causing it to seek revenge?

I retreated a step until my go-bag bumped against the wall. But when a head emerged next, the "branches" affixed to its crown, I realized it wasn't an infernal dryad at all.

It was Herne.

He continued to sit up, the dogs alternately nosing him and leaping away in apparent agitation. I recognized his jerkin—it was the same brown suede with the gold embroidered insignia as the "metaphorical" one that Grizel had hung on the tree. For a guy with a twenty-four point rack on top of his head, he looked relatively human-average, if on the large side, although his face was gaunt, his cheekbones pronounced, and his closed eyes sunken. He definitely looked ill. His skin, which probably was a medium brown when he was at his best, was taupe, bordering on gray.

Then it hit me. He and the *Cwn Annwn* had been stuck here for a minimum of three days. According to Zeke, demon overlords never bothered to allow their minions food or water because demons didn't need them. Herne and the pack weren't demons, and if regular meals weren't on their captors' radar, they probably hadn't had anything to eat and drink since they'd landed here.

"Herne?" I croaked.

Every single dog in the place swiveled their head to stare at me as Herne opened his eyes. If I hadn't already been plastered against the wall, I would have backed up, because Herne's eyes were the same glowing gold as the *Cwn Annwn*, as Doop's. I suspected I could take my Sheol-goggles off and see just fine in the light they cast.

Except Herne's eyes were fading like a dying flashlight. Jeez, what had they done to him to get him in here?

"What are you?" he rumbled, his voice deeper than Lachlan's. "You appear human, but never have I encountered a human with a tail."

"A tail?" I glanced down. "Oh." Lachlan's cable was trailing down my thigh. "Not a tail." I unhooked the carabiner. "See?" I coiled the cable and laid it on the floor.

"Ah. My mistake." His eyes drifted closed, and he listed to one side. I suspect he would have fallen if there hadn't been three or four dogs propping him up.

"Herne? Sir? If you don't mind my saying, you don't look so good. I have some water and some energy bars. Will your hounds object if I bring them to you?"

He perked up at that. "They will not harm you." His eyes narrowed as he peered at Doop. "How have you come by a *Ci Annwn*, and such a young one at that?"

"Uh, long story." I eased the go-bag off my back. "I'll tell you after you have something to eat and drink."

He waved one hand and the *Cwn Annwn* parted like a red-eared sea. I crept toward where he sat, and when I hunkered down next to him, I noted that he was wearing leather pants identical to the ones Jordan had worn out of Faerie. I unzipped the bag and winced. While Zeke had over-packed for a quick trip to Sheol—half a dozen bottles of water and as many energy bars—the supplies wouldn't be adequate for a double-extra-large meta-god and his attendant pooches. However, it was all that we had, so I pulled out one water bottle and uncapped it.

"Drink this."

He accepted the bottle with an incline of his head and I had to dodge the horns to avoid getting a point in the eye. Instead of drinking, though, he dumped water into his hand and held it out to the nearest dogs.

"Herne. Sir. Your Huntership. I really think you need to drink something yourself."

"No hunter worth his prey sups before his beasts."

"Yeah, but—" When Herne flashed those glowing eyes at me, I gave up and helped distribute the water. The dogs were very well-behaved, only lapping once or twice before moving aside for the next. All of them had at least a doggy sip by the time the last bottle was nearly empty. I made Herne finish it off, though.

"You won't be any use to them if you're too weak to get out of here."

His thin lips lifted in what could pass for a smile if I wasn't too particular. "My weakness is immaterial as I cannot depart."

Frowning, I pulled out the energy bars and handed a couple to him so we could distribute pieces to the pack. "Why not?"

"Even were the threshold not warded, I know not where we are."

"Oh. That. We're in Sheol. In one of those pocket dimensions."

His eyebrows rose toward the tangled brown curls on his forehead. "Sheol? Ah. That explains much. The nature of such hideaways is like unto Faerie. One must know where one is and where one wishes to be before one can make the journey." He eyed me speculatively. "I shall not ask how a human came to bide in such a place."

"I'm not, er, biding. Just on a visit. Looking for you and the pack, as a matter of fact." I broke another energy bar into bits. "How did *you* come to...bide here?"

Pink washed his pale cheeks. "I would rather not say."

I sighed. "Look. Your disappearance is kind of a big deal, and a whole bunch of people are going to a lot of trouble to find you. For reasons." I dusted crumbs off my palms as Doop crept to my side and rested his head on my shoulder. "I really need the whole story so I know how to proceed."

His expression was part irritation, part embarrassment. "I was...to meet a man. For a tryst."

My jaw sagged. "A tryst? You mean like a date? In *Sheol*?"

"What fool would seek an assignation in Sheol?" he snapped. "I availed myself of one of those...those *apps*. We were to meet at a secluded bower in the open lands in Faerie." His shoulders sagged. "Although I was a fool indeed, for while I awaited my paramour, I was set upon and rendered insensible. I awoke here."

Okay, this guy's vocabulary needed a serious update. I suspected he'd be a big hit at Ren Faires, but not so much on Grindr. "You took your entire pack with you to your...tryst?"

The irritation returned. "Of course not. They arrived after I found myself ensconced in this prison." He glanced up at the rusting roof. "Although it appears the prison is smaller than once it was."

"It's shrinking?" I thought of the crumbling bricks in the antechamber. "Crap, it really is disintegrating. We've got to get out of here."

"I told you. I cannot pass the wards, and nor can my hounds. No one can, so your presence remains a mystery."

"Oh, that wasn't my doing, precisely. It was Doop."

Herne's impressive brows drew together. "To whom are you referring?"

"Oh. Sorry." I patted Doop's back. "This guy. We call him Doop because—another long story, and doesn't really matter. The point is, he detected the pocket threshold and actually made it through." I rubbed my elbow, which still ached from barking it on the crumbly vestibule wall. "And dragged me along with him."

"Ah. No doubt he sensed the presence of his pack mates." Herne shrugged one shoulder. "Where one wishes to go is not always defined by lake or meadow or hill. One may also focus on a being, or that being's nature." He pushed his tumbled curls off his forehead. "It is how I track my prey."

The light dawned. "That must be why they killed Sawyl. Without a…a locus, the dogs would be unable to escape."

Herne straightened, his eyes blazing. Literally. "Sawyl is dead?"

I grimaced. "Sorry, but yeah."

I was surprised flames didn't shoot out Herne's nose from the way his breath was sawing. "How dare those miscreants hurt him?" He glared at me. "Make no mistake. He shall be avenged."

"By Grapthar's Hammer," I murmured. Herne left off the fiery glare and bent his horned head toward me.

"What?"

"Never mind." But I made a mental note to add *Galaxy Quest* to my supe cultural immersion movie night agenda. I had to swallow thickly. Because unless we came up with a way to get out of this pocket before it collapsed completely, I'd never have those movie nights. Or any nights at all.

But I had a plan now: Herne's pack might not have an external locus, but Doop? He *so* did.

I cleared my throat. "Um...there's something else I should mention." I flicked a finger at his chest. "Your clothes. We found Grizel hanging them out to dry in Faerie a few days ago."

"Grizel? *You* tarried with Grizel?"

I bristled a little. Did he have to sound so disbelieving? "Yeah. It, um, wasn't my finest hour, and we ended up carrying your metaphorical trousers and jerkin away with us afterward."

He shook his head, the nearby dogs neatly dodging his horns. "I cannot believe you escaped unscathed." He sighed, glancing around. Had the walls gotten closer, the ceiling lower? "Grizel's handiwork foretells a violent end, not this slow wasting away like last year's wildflowers. I would almost prefer that quickness."

"Hey. None of that talk. We're getting out of here." Because I still hadn't kissed Lachlan Brodie, and no way was I giving up on that, no matter how dire the situation. "You said wards, but Doop and I had no trouble getting in."

"It is not the getting in, but the getting out." He gestured toward the wall where the tunnel entrance gaped. "Rue, St. John's wort, and salt. We cannot pass."

Hmmm. "Excuse me a minute?" The dogs had quit pacing now that they'd had a little snack and had settled down in a rough circle around Herne. I stood, picked my way through them, and hunkered down to study the floor by the tunnel mouth. There was definitely a line of herbs and salt there. I'd disarranged it a little when I'd crawled through. I brushed it aside, clearing it away with no trouble.

But then, I was human. Wards against supernatural threats didn't work on me. For the second time in less than an hour, my nature had turned out to be an advantage rather than a drawback.

I beckoned to Herne. "Could you come here a minute, please?"

His brow knotted, but he stood—and wow, those horns made a tall guy even taller. Maybe not as tall as Frang, but definitely up there. The dogs parted in front of him like trees before Eleri.

I pointed to the cleared threshold. "Voila. No wards."

His golden eyes widened. "How?"

"Human, remember? Think you can pass now?"

He lifted an eyebrow and pointed to his rack. "I fear the passageway is too small for me now. But if you could spirit my hounds to safety, I shall be forever grateful, even as I remain here to face my fate."

I glared—at a meta-god, which might be just as idiotic as hunting down Grizel, but desperate times, you know? "I *said* none of that talk." I reached toward one of his prongs but didn't touch it. "I've gotta ask. Horns or antlers?"

Herne blinked at me, and for a moment, he looked nearly as innocent as Jordan. "What?"

"Are those horns or antlers? Horns are permanently attached. Antlers are shed every year. Do you shed yours?"

He nodded. "Once the Wild Hunt rides and our prey is dispatched."

"Then shed 'em now."

He drew himself up. "I have never done such a thing."

Honestly, supes and their resistance to change. "If you're master of the Hunt and the entire population of hellhounds, surely you can master your own freaking headgear."

For an instant, I thought I'd gone too far. Herne was a force of nature, after all. But then he bowed his head, shoulders tensing, and his antlers clattered to the floor, causing Doop and the rest of the pack to leap away and whine.

Herne gazed up at me, his expression almost sheepish. "They have never seen me without them. I do not emerge between

Samhain and Beltane unless the horn sounds, and that triggers" —he inclined his head—"*antler* growth."

"Aces." A chunk of the righthand wall crashed to the floor and the roof groaned, losing another couple of feet in height. Dammit, we had no time to lose. "Here's what we'll do. Doop and I will crawl through first, and then—"

A thump in the vestibule accompanied a muffled, "Gabriel's *balls*."

"Will you *look* at this place?" Another voice, this one decidedly peevish. "Three days ago, it was six times this size."

Since none of my companions had ever visited this particular pocket or invoked Gabriel's naughty bits, I brilliantly deduced that we'd been joined by Herne's kidnappers.

Who were undoubtedly also murderers.

CHAPTER TWENTY-ONE

Around us, all the hounds, including Doop, began to growl. Herne's eyes lit like twin lanterns and his antlers started to sprout. *Uh oh.* We needed to hurry this along before these hunting instincts screwed us all.

I held my finger to my lips and drew my other hand across my throat. To his credit, Herne got the picture and stood down. Sort of. Although his antler nubs grew another inch.

"Augh!" That was the first guy. "That dreadful noise! Are you sure they can't get to me?"

"It's always about you, isn't it?" Peevish Guy was clearly as fed up with his companion as he was with the pocket's state. "The threshold of the inner chamber is warded. You're safe."

"So you say. *You're* not the one in chains." Sure enough, metal rattled, and it didn't tinkle merrily like Lachlan's chill suit. "They're humiliating. And they *chafe*. I should never have been subjected to this. I'm an *angel*."

Athaniel. It had to be. Not only was he the only prisoner currently not accounted for, but the jerk believed his position in the former Angelic Host made him a superior being with carte blanche to torment Zeke all day, every day. Figures he still hadn't stopped complaining.

"Will you shut up?" the other guy said. Yeah, I wasn't the only one who was over Athaniel's whining. "You know why it's necessary. Everyone must believe you're still imprisoned." He made a disgusted sound, followed by a sharp double thunk as if he'd tossed a rock and it had bounced once. "But this is unacceptable. This...this *shrinkage*. The gold I've lost. Hundreds, maybe thousands. *Hundreds* of thousands. And that's not counting whatever...*depreciation* is occurring in the main cavern. Why didn't you tell me those dratted hounds exuded cold? They're destroying the structural integrity of this pocket."

I glanced down at Doop and the other hounds. They were *supposed* to be cold? Weird.

"I didn't know, did I? You're the one who wanted to pen them up. So if it's anybody's fault, it's yours. Besides, what does it matter?"

"Matter?" Peevish Guy spluttered. "I told you. Hundreds, if not—"

"Yeah, yeah." I could *hear* Athaniel's eyeroll. "So you're losing money. So what? It's not like you ever *do* anything with it except count it, and you can always get more. But I have a *calling. A purpose.*"

Great. If there was anything worse than an avaricious asshole out to increase his wealth, it was somebody with a *cause*. Because you couldn't argue with the second and the first would *never* believe they had enough.

"Purpose." Peevish Guy's tone was laced with disgust. "Your only purpose is yourself."

"As it should be! I'm an *angel*. The true order is violated when I am degraded in this unjust fashion." Athaniel rattled his chains again. "But at least *he* is back in Sheol, where he belongs. Soon *he* will be the one in chains and I will return to my rightful place."

My jaw clenched. I had a really bad feeling about who *he* was. Athaniel's fall had been a direct result of his efforts to undermine Zeke, and the former angel was not the kind of guy to accept the consequences of his own actions when it was so much easier to blame somebody else.

"Whatever," Peevish Guy said.

"Gabriel's balls, Melchom, just let this infernal place *implode*," Athaniel spat. *Melchom*. Zeke's former supervisor and the *other* person who'd mistreated him. My ears started to burn, a sure sign my anger was about to get the better of me. "So you lose some gold. At least that hunter freak and his revolting beasts will be gone. And then we'll have leisure to bring our glorious plan to fruition, eliminating all demon infestations where they dare to nest. Offices," he said, disgust dripping from his words. "Hospitals. *Dance studios*. It's completely unacceptable."

"How exactly will we finance this glorious plan without more gold? This is one of the last pockets that the auditors haven't logged. You really think we can pull this off without the bribe money? You've already committed more than 100% of our total capital."

"That's the beauty of it," Athaniel crowed. "I've only contracted with *demons*. And once we succeed, all of them will be back *here*, and I will ascend once more to Elysium. None will be able to reach me to claim their share."

Unbelievable. I mentally added *The Producers* to my ever-growing movie night must-sees, not that I'd ever invite these jokers. In fact, they were about to go down. Hard.

Okay. Reality check? I was a human with a magical camera lens and the ability to sweep up weaponized herbs. Was I seriously about to confront the two supernatural powers who'd tormented Zeke forever?

You bet your ass I was.

I leaned closer to Herne so I could whisper to him under cover of the dogs' growls. "Can you get the *Cwn Annwn* to stay put until needed?"

"They do as I will."

"Even if you ask them to remain here without you?"

"Aye. They are well-trained." He eyed Doop, who was lying on the floor with his head propped on my camera bag. "Most of them."

"Don't worry about Doop. Just tell the main pack to wait until you call them." I retrieved Lachlan's cable and handed the free end to Herne. "Get a good grip on this. Don't let go, not for anything. Can you do that?"

"Verily."

Brother. "Right. I'm gonna crawl back with Doop and confront these assholes. When I give you the high sign, you join me and grab onto my belt." I pointed to the back of my jeans, where Lachlan had hooked the carabiner. "Here. And no taking revenge yet. Okay?"

His eyes blazed once more. "These are the varlets who killed Sawyl, are they not?"

"Yeah. I'm pretty sure. But there's more at stake, and we need them to keep breathing for a little longer." I stared him down, flaming eyeballs and all, until he finally nodded. "Good. Things will probably happen pretty fast at that point, so don't lose your hold on either the cable or me. I don't want to risk leaving you behind, because I have a feeling this will only work once." I took a deep breath. "Here goes nothing."

I didn't bother retrieving the go-bag—Zeke could replace it in a heartbeat—but I eased my camera bag out from under Doop's head and pushed it ahead of me into the tunnel, although the carabiner in my hand made crawling awkward. As I hoped, Doop was unwilling to stay behind and followed at my heels.

Athaniel and Melchom were still bickering and didn't even notice me until I stood up and shouldered my camera bag, Doop scrambling out after me. Athaniel, despite his blond, Abercrombie-model beauty, was looking a little worse for wear, his toga stained and ragged. Melchom, on the other hand, looked like a refugee from a mashup of *Downton Abbey* and *What We Do in the Shadows*.

When they finally registered us, they both gaped, reminding me strongly of Blair's first catch. "Hello, boys," I said cheerfully as I wound Doop's leash around my fist. "Fancy meeting you here."

"*You*," Athaniel growled.

Melchom frowned at him. "You know him?"

"This *human* knows about us. He consorts with Ozul-y-Kalon."

"Actually, I leave all the consorting action to Zeke's boyfriend. I'm just a co-worker. And a friend." I rocked back on my heels, pretending an ease I didn't feel. "I've gotta ask, guys, what's with all the prank calls to Quest? Seems a little petty for a demon overlord and his minion."

"I'm not a *minion*. I'm an *angel*." Athaniel sniffed. "And it served Ozul-y-Kalon right. He's gotten above his station. Better to keep him occupied until he's back here." He rattled his shackles. "In chains, as he should be."

Melchom ignored Athaniel as he studied me, his head tilted to one side and a sly smile on the nearly lipless mouth below his snout. "A human at large in Sheol with his soul intact?" His eyes lit, but with red instead of gold. "And unless I much mistake the matter, a desperate yearning to be worthy of the selkie king. Delicious!"

Dammit. The demon ability to detect desires made Zeke an extremely efficient office manager, but it was awkward bordering on devastating when facing his former supervisor.

I lifted my chin, forcing myself to meet those glowing eyes. "That's none of your business."

"No?" Melchom strolled a little closer, and since Athaniel's chains were tethered to a steampunkish gauntlet on his wrist, Athaniel stumbled closer too. "What would you give to have the selkie by your side?" Melchom's smile widened into a grin with altogether too many teeth. "Not as human, but as a supe? Shall we say..." He tapped the side of his snout with one manicured claw. "A grizzly shifter, perhaps? I assure you, for the right price, all can be arranged. Shall we negotiate?"

So he was offering me not only Lachlan, but a chance to be like Ted, *with* Ted, too? Full membership in the supe community with bonus choice of booty call? *Damn*, this guy was good. And what can I tell you? I was tempted. *So* tempted.

"You've got nothin', Melchom," I said, channeling Mal-level bravado for all I was worth. "Soul-collection is illegal now. The Realm Accords—"

Melchom waved that away with a negligent claw. "Details. Once the proper order is restored, certain records can be expunged or conveniently lost. Nobody needs to know."

Me. *I'd* know. I couldn't identify the feelings swirling in my middle, so I buried my hand in Doop's fur just to have something to hold onto, something to keep me anchored.

"Think of it," Melchom continued, his tone even and almost hypnotic, "all demons—including the dynastic 'cubi—returned to Sheol where they belong. Consider the opportunities."

I was. All the opportunities were on Melchom's side, on Athaniel's side. What about the opportunities that would be stripped from Zeke, from his friend at the hospital, from any other member of the Host making their way in the Upper World at last, or those who were working so hard to reorganize Sheol for a modern world?

And Ted… I had to swallow, wishing I'd reserved a mouthful of water. He was so happy with Quentin he practically glowed. Sure, Quentin had scared the pants off me the first time I'd met him, and I'd been jealous of his place in Ted's life for a long time, but he was a good man—good incubus, I guess. He did good work, *important* work in the community. I didn't wish him gone, nor did I want Ted's joy to be diminished by one iota just because these two assholes had delusions of grandeur.

It hit me then, not like a smack to the head, but like the bloom of an *Aha!* flower expanding in my chest. And let me tell you, if there wasn't such a thing in Faerie, Sheol, or any other realm? There *should* be, because it was freeing and uplifting and goddamn *magical*.

I didn't want *Ted*. I wanted Ted's *happiness*, and not from inside it, if that makes sense? I was content to observe it, to stand by and rejoice in it. As his *friend*.

Because being his friend was enough. Being his friend was a *gift*. Being his friend was something I never wanted to lose, just as I didn't want to lose Zeke, or Quentin, or... Could I say it? Could I mean it? Why yes. Yes I could, even though it took a trip or two to hell for me to realize it.

I didn't want to lose my humanity.

Because every now and then—like when I'd brushed aside the wards that kept Herne trapped—being human was my superpower.

I was MattHugh, with a foot in both camps. And whether they admitted it or not, the supe community needed me to be their Jiminy Cricket. To remind them that change should be embraced, that *different* didn't mean *lesser*, that they should aspire to be *better*, and that they had limits too.

Melchom, for instance, wasn't as all-seeing as he liked to think. Because I already had my true desire: surrounded by true friends, building a life with a man like Lachlan, working at Quest, and discovering more about the supe community every day. What more could I possibly want?

Athaniel tugged on his chain. "Melchom, we're wasting time. Eliminate this human so we can be on our way."

Melchom scowled at the whiny ex-angel. "If you persist in wasting resources in this fashion, I will seriously reconsider our partnership."

"You can't!" Athaniel cried. I knew what was coming next so I mouthed it along with him when he proclaimed, "I'm an angel!"

Before they could engage in another bickerfest, I drawled, "You make an intriguing offer, Melchom. But I never make decisions without advice."

"Advice?" Melchom chuckled. "Who would you trust with so fundamental a choice?"

"Oh, I don't know. Maybe...*Herne!*" I shouted his name, and Herne burst out of the tunnel and to his feet before the echo died.

Athaniel screamed, and retreated as far from Herne as his chains allowed, which pulled them taut and nearly rocked Melchom off his cloven hooves. "No, no, no!"

I glanced up at Herne. "You know that guy?"

Herne bared his teeth. "He was my *date*."

"Dude," I said to Herne, "you could do *so* much better."

"*He could not!*" Athaniel shrieked. "Just the notion that I'd stoop to even *touch* someone like *him*. I'm an *angel*."

"Not anymore, jackass," I said, and lunged forward, snapping the carabiner around the chain stretched between Melchom and Athaniel. "Doop! Find Jordan!"

I didn't have to ask Doop twice. He took two lolloping steps and leaped, yanking me through the air behind him, Herne behind me, and—if the startled yelps were any indication—Melchom and Athaniel behind him.

Straight at the crumbling wall.

CHAPTER
TWENTY-TWO

Thank goodness for aramid cable, supernatural hound strength, and Doop's unending devotion to Jordan, because we landed in the nexus cavern in a clatter of claws and chains.

"Doop!" Jordan cried. "You're all right!"

"I am too, thanks." I managed to free myself from Doop's leash before he yanked my arm off in his eagerness to reach Jordan where he stood halfway across the cavern along with Lachlan, Niall, Zeke, and a tall guy with flaming hair—and I mean literal fire, not just ginger locks.

As Athaniel whimpered and whined behind me and Melchom tried to drag him into the *Sauna, Payroll, Ice & Vending (Out of Order)* tunnel, I turned to Herne. "Call the pack. Now. Before the pocket collapses any further."

Herne stuck two fingers in his mouth and whistled louder than the factory horn in *Sweeney Todd*. Before I could even blink, white, red-eared hounds were leaping out of midair. The instant their paws touched the ground, they headed for Melchom and Athaniel, circling them with growls loud enough to shake the stalactites overhead.

Before I could turn around, I was enveloped in a tight, silvery embrace. "I've got you, lad," Lachlan murmured in my ear. "You're safe now, never fear."

Don't get me wrong, being wrapped in Lachlan's arms was exactly where I wanted to be, although probably with fewer onlookers, no hellhounds, and a little natural light. But Lachlan's words struck me as...off.

I turned in the circle of his arms until I could face him. "I know." I pointed at the cable, which was still attached to Athaniel's chain. "I told you Shirl knows what she's doing."

His brow pleated. "The cable? But it failed. Or I failed, not keeping my hold on it." He laid a big, callused palm against my cheek. "I'm sorry. But I've made it right."

"Made what right?" It was hard to see his eyes clearly through two sets of Sheol-goggles. "It worked out perfectly. Without the cable, I wouldn't have been able to pull Herne out."

His frown deepened. "*You* pulled Herne out? But—"

"Well, well, well." The flame-haired guy sauntered over to us, tossing something from hand to hand, and I realized I knew him: Paimon, a high Sheol muckety-muck and the demon overlord who'd hauled Athaniel away for punishment in the first place. "Isn't this interesting?"

"Paimon. Sir. Your Excellency," I said, wondering if I should kneel or bow. But you know what? Screw it. I stayed on my feet, although I might have leaned against Lachlan just a little.

"You may address me as Auditor General, my good human," he said with a wink before turning to glare at Melchom and Athaniel. "According to my investigation, you two have been very naughty boys." He clucked his tongue, which...was it? Yep, it was forked. "Lucifer was extremely annoyed over your little scheme to siphon off power and gold that by rights belong to him as CEO and president of our board."

"Holy crap," I muttered. These guys were trying to stage a hostile takeover from *Lucifer*? They weren't just egotistical, arrogant, and homicidal. They needed freaking brain transplants.

"I did nothing wrong," Athaniel cried. "I'm working for the true order, the greater good." Just then, he caught sight of Zeke, who was standing behind Niall's shoulder. "*You*. This is all *your* fault."

Despite the *Cwn Annwn* surrounding him, Athaniel launched himself toward Zeke, but before he'd gone two feet, a green object whizzed through the air and struck him square on the nose.

"Ow!" He clapped his hands to his face. Blood dripped between his fingers to patter on the stone floor, much to the hounds' interest. One of them nosed the green object at Athaniel's feet.

It was a Frisbee.

I turned to Jordan, whose hands flexed at his sides, his expression half proud and half anxious. "*Damn*, Jordan. Nice shot."

He shrugged. "I throw Frisbees, too, even though mostly I catch them, or, you know, bury them or chew them." His eyes widened. "When I'm a *wolf*, not when I'm humanish. Jeez, my dentist would *kill* me." Then he smiled brightly. "Welcome back, Hugh. We were so worried, but then Lachlan made his deal, and —"

"Wait. What?" I pulled out of Lachlan's arms. "What deal?"

"The deal to get you back, of course," Lachlan said with no hint of apology.

"You didn't need to make any deal for that. I got back myself. *With* Herne, and in pretty good time, too, if I do say so myself."

"But, Hugh," Jordan said, "you were gone for hours and *hours*."

I frowned. "No I wasn't. Half an hour. Forty-five minutes, tops."

Niall shook his head. "Afraid not. We were almost at the end of our safety window. We were debating whether we should stay longer"—he raised an eyebrow at Lachlan, who huffed— "when Paimon arrived."

"Yes, wasn't it fortuitous?" Paimon buffed the object in his hand against his Hunter's Moon T-shirt. He held it up, and it gleamed like red fire in his hand. "I've always had a weakness for rubies."

I rounded on Lachlan. "You traded him the selkie crown *jewels*?"

"Just the one, lad."

"But it wasn't *necessary*. I got out on my own."

"How do you know?" Paimon purred. "Perhaps I put your entire escape plan in your head."

Zeke dodged out from behind Niall. "You didn't. You know you didn't. You don't have that kind of power, and even if you did, it would negate any contracts resulting from the action. All participants must sign of their own free will." He glared at Paimon. "You *cheated* Lachlan."

Paimon spread his hands, one still cradling the ruby. "The contract only specified that the human would be freed, not by whom. I believe you'll find that the *No Refunds* policy is clearly stated in the fine print."

Zeke's fury was almost palpable. "You—"

"Of course," Paimon said smoothly, "if Mr. Brodie wishes to request arbitration, he's within his rights. Although there is such a distressing backlog at the moment that you all could be waiting for quite a while."

"Nay," Lachlan said, tucking me close to his side again. "I'll not contest our agreement. I have Matthew back, and that's worth any cost."

My heart squeezed in my chest. "Lachlan," I said, my voice broken and hearts probably floating over my head. Honestly, this guy...

"You two can bill and coo later," Niall said. "We need to get back topside before our time is up."

I pointed at Melchom and Athaniel, who were still captives of the *Cwn Annwn*. "You'll make sure they're punished? They murdered the kennel master and kidnapped Herne and his pack."

Paimon narrowed his eyes at the prisoners. "Is this true?"

"It was for the greater good!" Athaniel said from behind his hands. Melchom just crossed his arms, rolling his eyes. Apparently, he wasn't quite as delusional as Athaniel.

"Lucifer's balls," Paimon muttered. "This one *never* learns. Don't worry. They'll be dealt with." He glanced at Herne. "If you don't mind remaining to press charges?"

"Not in the least," Herne replied.

"Good," I said, looking from Lachlan to Niall to Zeke to Jordan, who was crouched next to Doop, his arm looped around the dog's neck. "Let's go home."

"One moment," Paimon said. "You're Matt Steinitz, am I right?"

"Yeeesss." I drew out the word in suspicion.

"I've seen your work. Your photographs are superlative."

"Um…thank you?"

"When we've got this lot settled"—he jerked his clawed thumb at Melchom and Athaniel—"perhaps I could hire you." He fluffed his, er, flames. "My headshot on the Sheol website could use a refresh."

I blinked at him. "Sheol has a website?"

"It does indeed." Paimon grinned, displaying sharklike teeth. "Just think of it as the really, *really* dark web."

CHAPTER
TWENTY-THREE

Our extended stay in Sheol wasn't without its effects. Although I'd wanted to haul Lachlan into my office for a little SFW private time, the instant we all stepped out of the portal in the Quest workroom, Bryce slapped us with a decontamination protocol that took ages.

Worse, because the spells were keyed to species, it meant we were all separated for the entire time.

When I finally emerged from mine, my hair still damp from the final shower, Niall was waiting for me in the corridor.

"Hugh. A moment, if you don't mind."

I glanced around, but there was no sight of Lachlan or anybody else in the curving fourth floor hallway. "Um, sure."

I followed him down two flights and into his office. He closed the door before perching on the front of his desk. I breathed a little easier. If he wasn't sitting *behind* the desk, then maybe his news wasn't too dire.

"You did excellent work, Hugh," he said. "You've earned a commendation and a bonus, as have Zeke and Jordan."

"Th-thank you."

"Also, I wanted to let you know..." He rubbed the back of his neck, a sign that he wasn't sure how his comments would be received. But at least he wasn't pinching the bridge of his nose.

"Go ahead, Niall. Whatever it is, I can take it."

"The complaints against you have been dropped."

I may have goggled at him for a good thirty seconds. "Dropped? Why?"

He smiled wryly. "It seems that you're god-touched."

"I'm what?"

"God-touched. Like me. Like Gareth. That gives you a certain immunity, but also a certain vulnerability."

I narrowed my eyes. "Just because Govannon poked me in the chest? So what does that mean?"

Niall's chest lifted in a sigh as he carded his fingers through his hair. "To be touched by a god means that you've passed a test that many never face." He grimaced. "Some tests are more difficult than others. Gareth and I...well, we had a much longer and more painful trial than you did when you ventured into the forge for the sake of others. But yours is no less meaningful. The god-touched occasionally get a pass that others don't."

"Like hiking around Faerie unescorted?" I asked hopefully.

He shrugged. "Among other things. Since Govannon was one of the blokes who created Faerie in the first place, his touch grants you full access. It doesn't mean you can take advantage of it to the extent it disturbs the residents, however."

"Am I still on probation?"

"Yes. But only for the remainder of your original term, not the additional year."

Score! I couldn't help my grin. "So what about the vulnerability part?"

Smirking, he quirked an eyebrow. "Your value as a spell ingredient just increased a thousand-fold."

My hands went cold. "Uh..."

"So try to toe the line and maybe stay out of random magic workrooms for a while?"

"Got it." I turned to go.

"And Hugh?"

I paused with my hand on the doorknob. "Yeah?"

"Maybe keep the...unusual properties of your telephoto lens on the down-low for now?"

My eyes widened. "You didn't tell the council that I can see invisible stuff?"

"No." He winked. "As long as we're engaged in locating the Disappeared, I wager we need all the secret weapons at our disposal."

I let go of the doorknob. "Do you suspect somebody is deliberately hiding the Disappeared?"

He shrugged. "Perhaps. Perhaps it's the Disappeared themselves who are hiding. But I don't want our hand forced, and I also don't want to alert anybody who might have their own reasons for perpetuating the losses. So for now? Mum's the word."

I nodded, and muttered, "Mum, mum, mum," in my best Thermian impression as I headed down the hall. *Galaxy Quest* was creeping up the movie night list.

When I rejoined everyone in the lobby—Zeke, Eleri, Jordan, and Doop, but no Lachlan, drat the luck—Eleri was perched on the stool next to Zeke's desk.

"Come on, Zeke, please? You used to be a matchmaker. Can't you find him a date?"

Zeke ducked his head. "I'm not in that business anymore."

I glanced between the two of them. "I hope you're not trying to find a date for *me*."

"As if," Eleri scoffed. "You're taken. I'm talking about Herne. He's clearly lonely if he was desperate enough to fall for Athaniel's fake dating app."

I raised my eyebrows. "It was fake?"

"Big time." She leaned forward, her forearms propped on her knees, her eyes sparkling. "Zeke got the whole story from Paimon after Melchom and Athaniel's trial. Athaniel never intended to let Herne anywhere near him, but he had to touch him to knock him out."

Zeke winced. "That stings. I know from experience."

"I think Herne was more hurt by the rejection than the kidnapping," I said. "Trying to find him a *real* date would be

E.J. RUSSELL

awesome. He's really not a bad sort for being the supe equivalent of the Lord High Executioner." I frowned. "But they kidnapped him before they murdered Sawyl, right?"

Eleri nodded. "That was Athaniel too, although Melchom was present."

"So without Sawyl and without Herne, how'd they capture the *Cwn Annwn*?"

Eleri chuckled. "Without a leader, the dogs fell back on instinct. They took off after their rightful prey."

I laughed too. "You mean the pack chased those goons all the way to Sheol?"

"They chased *Athaniel*. Which apparently was a huge surprise to him, because he assumed they'd go after Melchom."

"That'll teach him to stand up their boss and murder their kennel master. I bet the words, '*I'm an angel!*' were uttered more than once during that chase." I glanced at the corner, where a remarkably subdued Jordan sat with his arm around Doop. "But the pack left Doop behind."

Jordan peered up at us from under his floppy brown bangs. "Will Herne take him back now?" His arm tightened and Doop licked his chin. "I don't want to think of him eating the flesh of traitors instead of sweet potato fries."

"Aw, honey." Eleri slipped off the stool and hurried over to sit next to him. "I doubt Doop considers Herne the leader of the pack. He's still with you, right?"

"Yeah." Jordan tugged on Doop's ear, causing the dog's eyes to go half-lidded in pleasure. "But what if Herne *makes* him go back? He's not really mine."

I sat in the chair on Jordan's other side. "You weren't there when I told Bryce what happened in that collapsing dimension. You know how we got out?" Jordan shook his head. "I told Doop to find *you*. And he did."

Jordan's eyes were suspiciously bright. "Really?"

"Absolutely. Furthermore, Herne made no attempt to call him to heel. I think he knows when one of his dogs switches allegiance, and he's not about to fight it."

Alarm flickered across Jordan's face. "Switching allegiance? You mean Doop's a *traitor*? Will Herne and the coon-whatever track him down?"

I patted his arm. "Doop never coursed with the pack, so he can hardly leave something he never joined. In fact, when it comes down to it, they left *him* behind."

"You needn't worry, laddie." Lachlan's deep rumble from the doorway made my heart bump sideways. He strolled over and stood next to me, close enough that his leg pressed against my thigh. "Herne's relinquished his claim to yon hellhound, subject to him finding a good home elsewhere."

"He's got a good home. My home. I mean the Dog House. And here, right?" Jordan babbled. "Nobody minds if he comes to work with me, do they?"

"You know, Jordan, when Herne and I were trapped in that dimension, he said something to me. He said that where someone wants to go isn't always a place. Sometimes it's a person." I waggled my hand. "Granted, I'm paraphrasing, because Herne talks like a Shakespearean understudy. But that's the gist. I think he recognized that *you're* Doop's home."

"Oh." Jordan's smile dawned. "That's okay then." He stood up. "Come on, Doop. Let's hit the Burgerville. It's time for some sweet potato fries!"

Dog and werewolf trotted out of the lobby and a moment later, the thump of footsteps and clatter of claws sounded on the stairs.

Eleri fluttered her eyelashes, her hands clasped under her chin. "A boy and his dog. So heartwarming." She slid off her chair. "If you'll excuse me, I've got a book club meeting."

Eleri's *book club* was actually a group of rebellious dryads. "What's today's selection? *Little House in the Big Woods*? *The Giving Tree*? *The Word for World is Forest*?"

"Shut up or I'll sic them on your Honda again, and I doubt you want to dig it out from under a ton of oak leaves and pine needles." She waggled her fingers. "See you guys later."

Lachlan watched her go, shaking his head as he chuckled. "She's a braw lass, and no mistake."

"You can say that again."

"No need," he said with a wink, and sat next to me.

I studied him out of narrowed eyes. "Do you really know that Herne's not seeking Doop's custody, or did you just say that to soothe Jordan's nerves?"

He shook his head. "You know better, lad. Selkies don't lie. I know because Herne told me."

"He did?"

"Aye. Asked for a wee chat after he paid a visit to Grizel and reclaimed his clothing."

I gaped at him. "He can do that?"

"Apparently. But only because you and your friends interrupted her in the first place." He reached into his anorak pocket and pulled out a tiny square of parchment. He smoothed it on his knee and then handed it to me.

It held two strings of numbers. "What's this?"

"The coordinates for Wyn's location. A lake west of Eugene belonging to a beaver shifter clan." He smiled, and I felt it all the way to my toes. "Herne passed it along to me."

"Uh...how'd he get it? And more to the point, why give it to you?"

"Since Wyn and I are severing the knot, some might see us as oath-breakers. Herne's rightful prey."

I scowled at the paper. "You're not. Not when you've reached a mutually satisfactory decision."

"Easy, lad." He patted my back. "It's enough to register on Herne's tracker senses, but not enough for him to set the hounds on us."

"Good to know," I muttered.

"As to why? Seems he feels he owes you a debt. In fact"—the smile morphed to a full-on grin—"he says you may call on him whenever you like, particularly if you keep the clothing you spirited away from Grizel safely locked up for good."

"I—" I had to clear my throat to get words out. "I can do that."

"So tell me, Matthew." Lachlan's voice, low and warm, zinged right down my spine. "I bought a new canoe. Will you come on a wee paddle with me to"—he tapped the parchment—"see the sights?"

I met his gaze, my mouth dry. "Is the canoe in your truck?"

"Aye."

"Is your truck outside?"

"It is," he said, a decided twinkle in his eye.

"Good." I grabbed his hand and towed him out of the office toward our future.

WHAT'S NEXT?

CHECK OUT MATT'S NEXT CASE!

THE LADY UNDER THE LAKE

This client is all wet...

After receiving a hot tip on the whereabouts of my almost-boyfriend's nearly-ex-husband (hey, I told you—it's complicated!), I thought my love life was finally coming up for air. But when we stake out the remote lake, it's not the ex who surfaces.

It's the Faerie King's long-missing mother (and I mean *really* long, as in double-digit centuries), and she wants to hire Quest Investigations. Since one of my bosses is the king's brother, he has a tsunami of...*feelings* about her as a potential client, and refuses to take the case. Instead, he passes it to me.

Yes! However...

Should I be thrilled at the vote of confidence or suspicious that he's tossing me in the deep end without a life preserver, the better to punish the woman who abandoned her kid all those years ago?

You know what? It doesn't matter. I may be Quest's token human, but I've proven I can get the job done, so I dive right in. Then the lady explains what she wants me to do: find her missing child.

Seriously? I expected more of a challenge. All I have to do is introduce her to the king and bingo, case closed. But when she says, *not* that *one*, this little family drama threatens to send ripples throughout the supernatural community—especially with my boss in over his head as the prime suspect in a fae kidnapping.

As if things weren't complicated enough... Remember that nearly-ex? When he shows up and muddies the waters, I'm faced with a choice: I can solve this case *or* I can finally hook my almost-boyfriend.

Dammit.

THE LADY UNDER THE LAKE

Lachlan took my hand and led me onto the dock, our footsteps echoing hollowly. When we got to the end, he sat down and patted the boards next to him. "Have a seat. We may need to wait for a bit before we get Wyn's attention." I complied, and when he pulled me tighter against his side, I didn't resist.

He withdrew a folded paper from his pocket and cupped it in both hands. After whispering something to it, he leaned over and let it flutter to the water.

I blinked at it. "Bryce gave you a paper boat?"

He chuckled. "What is it you human folk say? It's not the form that's important. It's the function. And I mind that your druid friend has a whimsical side to his nature."

That was true. Bryce had once configured a paintball tagger to deliver an anti-evil potion. I sighed as we watched the little white boat bob on the gentle swells, moving away from the dock as though it had an invisible paper motor. About ten feet out, it began to spin like it was caught in a tiny whirlpool and got sucked beneath the surface.

"Guess the message doesn't require a signature for delivery," I muttered.

Beside me, Lachlan uttered an odd sound, half cough, half hum, half throat-clearing. Okay, so fractions aren't my strong suit, but you get the picture. "Matthew."

When he didn't continue, I turned my head to look at him. He was staring out over the water, his brow knotted, and my belly felt as though it was caught in that same mini-whirlpool. "Yes?"

"After Wyn surfaces, I won't be able to...be with you."

"Ah." The whirlpool spun faster. "I understand." But I didn't. Not really.

He must have caught my mood because he turned and took my hands, his face earnest in the sunlight reflecting off the lake. "Not forever. I don't mean that. But he and I will have meetings with the King's seneschal, with last affidavits to file and scheduling to finalize. Until we face the King and he severs our knot, our sundering won't be official." He smiled crookedly. "And I believe I've mentioned that I can't trust myself alone with you for too long."

The light dawned and my stomach stopped doing pirouettes. "Is that why you drove into town today? Why you brought Blair with you?"

"Aye. When Herne was able to give us Wyn's whereabouts, it got me thinking. I'll not risk your safety, not put you on the Wild Hunt's radar, even by association." His jaw tightened. "I'll not have our joining tainted by the least hint of wrongdoing."

I squinted at him. "When you say joining, do you mean *joining*? As in"—I gestured between us—"*joining*?"

His expression softened. "I do. In all senses of the word."

"Oh." I was trapped in that hot, dark gaze. "That's, um, good." Surely one kiss wouldn't be *that* risky. Lachlan's breath wafted over my cheek, my lips. *It's finally going to happen.* I leaned in, my eyelids fluttering as I closed that last. Critical. Inch.

And fell over sideways, because Lachlan surged to his feet. "Look!"

He pointed at the center of the lake, beyond where the boat had vanished. At first, as I pushed upright again, heat burning my cheeks above my beard, I thought he was just deflecting. Redirecting to cover his sidestep of my awkward lunge, because all I could see was bright sunlight reflecting off the greeny-blue water. But when I squinted against the glare, I realized the buttery yellow glow was coming from *below* the surface.

I pushed aside my embarrassment and scrambled up to stand next to Lachlan. This was it! After almost two months of waiting and wondering, we were about to face Wyn again. I wasn't entirely sure whether I'd want to hug him or sock him when he showed up, because leaving Lachlan—and me—hanging was kind of a jerk move. But then, Wyn had been magically roofied by his douchebag of an ex-boyfriend, so I couldn't entirely blame him for wanting some space.

Lachlan fumbled for my hand, and I clutched his, almost leaning over the water as the glow floated closer...closer... closer. As it brightened, the dock began to vibrate, shivering on its pilings in time with an arhythmic drumming.

Then a furry white figure the size of a small pony shot by us, sending me stumbling against Lachlan. It landed in the lake with a massive splash that drenched the front of my jeans.

Lachlan wiped water off his face. "Is that—"

"It is," I said resignedly, as an enormous white dog with red ears flailed in the water in front of the dock. "Our very own hellhound." Which meant—

"Doop!" Jordan Tate, Quest's werewolf intern, raced down the dock to teeter on its edge until Lachlan grabbed his giant backpack to steady him. "Not the *water*. The *selkie*." He shot a grin at us. "Hi, Hugh! Hi, Lachlan. Sorry about the mess."

"Okay, Jordan. I'll ask the obvious question. Why are you here?"

"We're working on his tracking skills," he said, his attention on Doop. "I told him to find Lachlan, but he's having a hard time separating the person from the place. I probably need to be a little more specific, huh?" He shrugged off his pack. "His aim is still a little wonky too, but we're working on that with some Frisbee therapy." Jordan kicked off his sneakers and shed his jacket.

When he unbuckled his belt, I said, "Hang on. What are you doing?"

He peered at me from under his floppy brown bangs. "I have to get him out of the water, obviously." He heaved a sigh as he looked at Doop, who was smacking the lake surface with his front paws in an extremely uncoordinated dog paddle. "Again."

"But you hate the water."

"I know. But Doop's my responsibility, so it's up to me, isn't it?" He shucked off his jeans, revealing a pair of *Avengers* briefs. "But that doesn't mean I want to walk around in wet clothes for the rest of the day." He smiled sunnily. "Good thing I started carrying extra underwear in my pack after the last three times."

"Laddie," Lachlan said, "yon hellhound must weigh twice what you do. You'll not be able to lift him out on your own."

"I'm a werewolf. We're stronger than we look."

Lachlan shook his head and reached for his belt buckle. "You'll need help."

"Whoa." I held my hands up in a timeout T. "Let's think about this a little, shall we?" I checked on Doop. He didn't appear to be in danger of drowning—the three of us were more threatened by the water he was flinging about than he was. Well, us and the lake's entire fish population. While he didn't look exactly ecstatic to be in the drink, he didn't look panic-stricken either. I pointed to the shore next to the dock. "Why not just call him from over there? Get him to come out on his own?"

Jordan froze with his hands on his T-shirt hem. "But he's not good at swimming." Understatement. "How can he get over there?"

I shrugged. "Entice him. Offer him a treat. It might take him a while, but he'll manage with the right incentive."

Jordan brightened. "That's a great idea, Hugh!" He caught the strap of his backpack and scampered up the dock in his T-shirt, socks, and briefs.

I sighed. "I suppose I should be grateful he didn't strip down completely this time."

Lachlan lifted that scarred eyebrow. "This time?"

"Long story." I poked him in the chest. "And don't pretend you weren't about to do the same."

"Just trying to help." He winked.

"Uh huh."

On the shore, Jordan unzipped the backpack and pulled out a Frisbee. Because of course he would.

"Here, Doop! Here, boy!" He waggled the bright green disk over his head. Doop uttered a yip and began thrashing toward the shore. "That's it. You can do it." Doop flailed harder, generating a veritable canine tsunami as he floundered toward shore.

When he finally heaved to his feet in the shallows and lolloped into Jordan's arms, I turned back to the lake.

The glow had vanished. Guess Wyn wouldn't be breaking the surface today after all.

Dammit.

A MESSAGE FROM
E.J.

Dear Reader,

Thank you so much for reading *The Hound of the Burgervilles*, the second book in my Quest Investigations mystery series! If you're curious about Matt's backstory, you might want to check out his debut on the Mythmatched stage in *Single White Incubus*, the first in the Supernatural Selection trilogy about a paranormal matchmaking agency, or his later appearance (along with Jordan's introduction) in *Howling on Hold*. If you'd like to go all the way back to the Mythmatched beginnings, the story world dawned with *Cutie and the Beast*, a paranormal rom-com where a cursed fae warrior turned psychologist clashes with his determined temporary office manager. As you might expect, hijinks ensue!

You can see all my books on my website, https:// ejrussell.com, or on my Amazon author page here: https:// www.amazon.com/author/ej_russell. Most are also available at Apple, Kobo, and Barnes and Noble.

Would you like exclusive content and ARC giveaways, not to mention gratuitous dance videos? Then I'd love for you to join me in Reality Optional, my Facebook fan group (https:// facebook.com/groups/reality.optional). My newsletter is the place to get the latest dish on new releases, sales, and more. I promise I only send one out when I've got...well...news. You can subscribe here: https://ejrussell.com/newsletter.

All my best,
—E

Death on Denial

Art Medium Series
The Artist's Touch
Tested in Fire
Art Medium: The Complete Collection (omnibus edition)

Legend Tripping Series
Stumptown Spirits
Wolf's Clothing

Enchanted Occasions Series
Best Beast
Nudging Fate
Devouring Flame

Royal Powers Series (shared world)
Duking It Out
Duke the Hall
King's Ex

Magic Emporium Series (shared world)
Purgatory Playhouse

Monster Till Midnight

Historical Romance
Silent Sin

Contemporary Romance
Camera Shy
The Thomas Flair
Mystic Man
For a Good Time, Call... (A Bluewater Bay novel, with Anne Tenino)

ABOUT THE
AUTHOR

E.J. Russell (she/her), author of the award-winning Mythmatched paranormal romance series, writes LGBTQ+ romance and mystery in a rainbow of flavors. Count on high snark, low angst, and happy endings.

Reality? Eh, not so much.

She's married to Curmudgeonly Husband, a man who cares even less about sports than she does. Luckily, C.H. also loves to cook, or all three of their children (Lovely Daughter and Darling Sons A and B) would have survived on nothing but Cheerios, beef jerky, and Satsuma mandarins (the extent of E.J.'s culinary skill set).

E.J. also writes traditional cozy mystery as Nelle Heran. She lives in rural Oregon, enjoys visits from her wonderful adult children, and indulges in good books, red wine, and the occasional hyperbole.

News & Social Media:
Website: https://ejrussell.com
Newsletter: https://ejrussell.com/newsletter

ACKNOWLEDGEMENTS

Many thanks to my awesome beta readers—Kelly Jensen, Lisa Leoni-Kinley, and lyric apted—for suggestions, advice, and encouragement; to Meg DesCamp for editing magic; to L.C. Chase for the adorable cover; to my family for endless support; and of course to you, my readers, for accompanying me on this wild journey.

Without all of you, I wouldn't be able to continue to do what I love.